"Have You Thought About My Offer?" Connor Asked.

"I didn't think you were serious," Eve replied.

"I was, most definitely." His eyes were focused on her face.

"Why would you want my house when you have *this* house?"

"Why would a *TV star* want to live on this side of the island?"

Eve frowned. "And everyone's got their price, right?"

His look sharpened. "What's yours?"

Her temper stirred and stretched. "You can't afford it."

For the first time she saw anger flare in his eyes. He definitely had not learned that he couldn't always have whatever he wanted....

Dear Reader,

When Princess Diana died, I stopped buying women's magazines. I hated the way they canonized her after being so relentlessly savage only days before. Nothing has changed. Superstars are born and then hacked off at the knees in public. These days, I catch up with the gossip in the supermarket queue and put the magazine back before I have to pay for it (a terrible admission for a writer.) I am heartily sick of the line "the public's right to know," and I find the methods of the paparazzi repugnant.

But many celebrities also use the magazines to promote themselves, for which they are well paid. So where do you draw the line?

The hero of this book shunned the limelight. But when it suited his cause he relented. Although in his case, perhaps he should have followed his instincts. I guess he is like most of us. We crave the spotlight for our own gratification or because we hope we can make a difference. But we don't necessarily want our mothers there, telling the world every detail of our bowel habits when we were three.

Best regards,

Jan Colley

JAN COLLEY

MELTING THE ICY TYCOON

Silhouette® Desire

Published by Silhouette Books

America's Publisher of Contemporary Romance

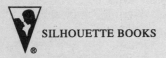 SILHOUETTE BOOKS

ISBN-13: 978-0-373-76770-0
ISBN-10:   0-373-76770-6

MELTING THE ICY TYCOON

Printed in U.S.A.

Books by Jan Colley

Silhouette Desire

Trophy Wives #1698
Melting the Icy Tycoon #1770

JAN COLLEY

lives in Christchurch, New Zealand, with her long-suffering fireman and two cats who don't appear to suffer much at all. She started writing after selling a business, because at tender middle age, she is a firm believer in spending her time doing something she loves. A member of the Romance Writers of New Zealand and the Romance Writers of Australia, she also enjoys reading, traveling and watching rugby. E-mail her at vagabond232@yahoo.com.

For Julie Broadbridge

You know grief better than I, my listening friend, and
still you bolster us all with your smile and optimism.
Where would we be without you?

One

Bang! Bang! Bang!

So hot...what is that noise?

"Hello! Anyone there?"

So tired...

Bang! Bang!

Eve reared into a sitting position, her heart pounding. Seconds behind, her mind drifted up through a handful of faraway voices and a swirling crescendo of Tchaikovsky.

And a tremendous thumping. Her upper body swayed in a dizzy spell. The banging continued.

Disoriented, she pushed to her feet. She'd fallen asleep on the couch. The fire had gone out but she was burning up.

"Hang on." It was the first she'd spoken in days and her throat was shocked into a coughing fit. She took just a couple of steps before she cracked her shin on one of the boxes still to be unpacked. Swallowing a swear word, she staggered toward the door.

"Who's there?" she called out.

"Your neighbor" came the terse reply.

Neighbor? Where was she? Oh, yes, the new house on Waiheke Island, where she'd moved a few days ago.

Eve leaned on the door, fishing in her pockets for a tissue. The knocking started up again, crashing through her head. She put her hands to her head—but that wasn't her hair, it was too short. Then Eve remembered. She had cut it off a couple of weeks ago. New beginning, new hair. Cut out the bad stuff—the divorce, losing her job—snip snip.

Bang! Bang! Bang!

"Coming…" The ancient key was stiff and her wrists weak as spaghetti but finally the door creaked open. Eve swayed with the exertion of the past two minutes, hot and sweaty under her baggy sweatshirt. Even her feet were hot in their thick striped socks.

She looked down. They were half-off, she thought with disgust, then was distracted by enormous shiny shoes and the scissor-sharp creases of slate-gray pants. The jacket matched the trousers. Her eyes roamed up the body—there was a lot of body. Legs that went on forever, the torso just as long but broad, too. Eve paused at her eye level, seriously woozy.

She moved her head back as far as she dared and zoomed in on a somber maroon tie around a lighter shade of smooth collar. Strong chin, wide lips with a definite bow in the center. Lovely green eyes frowned out of a high, wide forehead. The whole attractive parcel was topped with an expensive cut of rich-brown hair, complemented by neat sideburns.

Funny how her mind was fogged with sleep and flu drugs, yet the stranger's features were indecently clear, as if molded in a lustrous gold.

"Whoa…" Eve succumbed to another dizzy spell. She lurched and caught the door frame.

The man snapped into action and steadied her arm. "Are you okay?"

"Don't!" she croaked.

He jerked his hand away but did not step back.

"Contagious," she added, holding the door frame with one hand. She dragged the tissue across her nose and wondered if it looked as raw as it felt.

The stranger appeared concerned but not friendly. At least, she thought, the way she looked and sounded, rape was probably not an option. And if murder was on his mind, she decided death would be a blessed relief.

He stared, and Eve waited for the shock of recognition.

"You're—Eve Summers."

"Drumm." She licked lips that felt like gravel. "Divorced." New beginning, new name. Technically new-old name, maiden name. Since the divorce was just a few weeks old, it took a bit of getting used to, even for her.

He squinted at her. "You look—different."

A growing pressure on the bridge of her nose indicated a potential sneeze. "My makeup crew and stylist aren't unpacked yet," she rasped.

He peered over her shoulder, frowning. The classical piece blaring out of the national radio program wound up to a revolutionary climax. "Have you seen a doctor?" The question was almost a shout.

Eve flinched. "It's flu." Standing in the chill of the open doorway was not helping, but she couldn't invite him in.

The place was a train wreck. She was a train wreck. "It just has to run its course."

Yet even loaded up with antihistamines, she could still appreciate a fine form of a man when she saw one.

"There are doctors in the village," he said.

"A doctor would only prescribe bed rest and fluids."

"And quiet, perhaps." He obviously did not like Tchaikovsky. "I saw you move in three days ago. Since then there has been no sign of life."

Eve's eyes were gritty and dry and she felt hollow. If she didn't sit down soon she would fall down. "Did you want something?"

Not the friendliest question for a new neighbor, but she would make it up to him some other time. Now she just wanted to be left alone to die in peace.

The man straightened, frowning at her lack of manners. "I was concerned," he said shortly.

He must be let down to see her like this, a million light-years from her normal public appearance. But Eve was barely surviving a bad enough couple of weeks without someone staring at her as if she was a bug he'd like to squash. "Look, I'd ask you in, but—" she gave a listless wave "—I haven't unpacked and the place is—" another wave "—and I'm—" dying, burning up, homicidal…take your pick.

His lips thinned and he snapped off a nod. "Before you unpack, I've come to make you an offer on the house."

The need to sneeze redoubled. She was so intent on keeping it in, she didn't answer.

"This house," he continued.

"This house?" Eve spread the fingers of both hands wide. He hadn't even told her his name and he wanted to buy her house?

"I will pay you," he said distinctly, "ten thousand dollars over what you paid for it."

Yeah, she was dreaming. Phew! So this gorgeous, expensively dressed man mountain is a figment of overactive imagination and a million milligrams of antihistamine taken a couple of hours ago—or was it yesterday?

She shook her head; it hurt.

"Ten thousand dollars is a tidy sum for no effort on your part."

"I just bought this house." The sneeze faded away and indignation pushed her voice up high, setting off another round of coughing.

He grimaced and leaned well back. "Twenty, then."

"If you wanted this place so badly, why didn't you make the old owner an offer?" She closed her eyes and silently begged him to go away and leave her alone.

Now he was almost glowering. "Let's just say Baxter and I did not see eye to eye on a lot of things."

"He turned you down?"

"He's a fool. I offered him twice the market value."

Eve shrugged. "Sorry."

The man made a sound of impatience. "Well then, I'm offering you twenty thousand over that to sell to me. Cash offer. No agent fees."

"Why would I buy a house one week and sell it the next?"

"Because you're smart. It's twenty grand for doing nothing."

She massaged her throbbing temples. The stranger handed her a business card, but the words on it phased in and out along with the thumping in her head. She swayed and bumped the door frame again.

"You need a doctor. Are you here on your own?"

"I just need sleep," she insisted, wishing he would take the hint and leave.

He stared at her for a few moments and then nodded. "Perhaps when you're feeling better." He took a step back.

Relief sparked a small spurt of defiance. "It won't be for sale then, either," she declared. Holding on to the door, she straightened her spine, proud of herself. Eve Summers—er, Drumm—was no pushover, sick or well.

And then the sneeze erupted in a shrill ah-choo! She covered her face with the damp tissue.

The man's eyebrows rose and she was mortified to see his mouth quirk in one corner. He then turned and strode off down the path.

"*My* path," Eve sniffed with satisfaction. She sank against the closed door and slid to the floor. The tissue in her hand was useless, but she could not gather the energy required to cross the room and replace it.

She looked down at the business card he'd pressed into her hand. Connor Bannerman. CEO of Bannerman, Inc. The name was vaguely familiar, but she was in no condition to trawl through the inflamed mush of her mind.

Sleep. Right here if necessary. She lifted her arm, and the crumpled card joined the general bedlam cluttering the floor of her new—old—house.

"Keep me informed." Conn stepped down from the container that doubled as a construction-site office cum tea room and raised a hand in farewell to his foreman. His face grim, he picked his way across the mud and gravel to the wire enclosure and the sleek corporate BMW waiting.

Damn and blast the council! They were well behind

schedule. He was tempted to pay a visit to the council offices himself and knock some heads together.

Conn Bannerman had been in the construction business for nearly a decade. In fact, he *was* the construction business in New Zealand, two states in Australia and now branching into the South Pacific. What he did not know about building requirements would fit on a postage stamp.

The council was messing him around. It was no secret that the incumbent mayor was opposed to the new stadium. He believed the city's money would be better spent elsewhere. And there was nothing Conn could do about it until the local body elections, just over a month away.

He opened the back door of the BMW and slid inside.

"The terminal, Mr. Bannerman?"

Conn nodded to his driver and slid his mobile phone from his overcoat pocket. He checked his messages and called the office.

"Pete Scanlon called about the fund-raiser on the twenty-fifth."

"Apologies," Conn told his secretary flatly.

"I sent them last week. He wants to make you some sort of presentation for sponsoring his campaign."

Conn grimaced.

"But I thanked him and said you had a prior engagement."

"Thank you, Phyll. I'll see you Monday."

"Don't forget…"

"The conference call with Melbourne tomorrow."

"At ten," the redoubtable Phyllis ended.

Conn wondered how he had ever managed without his awesome secretary. But for her, he would be in the office seven days a week instead of having the freedom to work from home when he chose.

He scowled and slid his phone back into his pocket. He would gladly work seven days a week for the biggest project of his life, but it wasn't going to plan. Pete Scanlon was his only hope, which was why Bannerman, Inc. was backing his campaign.

"Monday at nine, Mikey." Conn buttoned up his overcoat and stepped out onto the accessway of the ferry terminal. Extracting a ten-dollar bill from his wallet, he joined the queue at the newsagent's. While he waited, his free hand rested on a stack of magazines and he looked idly down.

She stared up from the glossy cover of a women's magazine. His fingers seemed to stroke her chin. He wondered why every time he saw that face, he could not stop looking.

She was not a stunning beauty, more your girl-next-door type—and wasn't that a joke? And, as he'd discovered, not nearly as attractive in person or as warm and gracious as she appeared on TV.

That was unfair, given her health at the time.

Her face was more round than heart-shaped and the hint of a double chin somehow added to the charm she projected on screen. The magazine's photographer had captured her eyes perfectly; the color of the harbor at dusk.

Why I Quit was the headline.

Conn's workload left him no time for gossip. But the hue and cry that had erupted when the country's top-rated anchor walked out of the studio a few weeks ago had permeated even his awareness. And now that hue and cry had landed virtually in his backyard.

Conn Bannerman had more reason than most to despise the media. Journalists, reporters, radio jocks—he wasn't picky when it came to labeling all of New Zealand's small media circle "scum." Before he met her, Eve Summers was the only one he might have given the time of day to. Her nightly current-affairs show was about the only time his wide-screen TV flickered into life, unless there was a rugby game on.

With a quick glance around, he opened the magazine and looked for the contents page and found the article.

"Burnout…a recent divorce—" He shook his head in disgust. That celebrities felt they must inflict their sad little problems onto anyone who would listen was bad enough. Why must the media also target people who desired nothing more than to keep their private lives private?

He sensed the customer in front moving and shoved the magazine forward a few inches.

"The usual, Mr. B.?"

He nodded at the *Business Review* beside the till and held out his money. *"Born Evangeline"*—pretty name, suited her. *"Her father dying…no other TV shows in the pipeline…single…"* Conn's eyes skimmed the article, picking out key words. The newsagent took the bill from his outstretched hand.

With a reluctant last look at the article, Conn closed the magazine, then inexplicably picked it up and laid it on a stack of papers by the till.

Two minutes later he was boarding the ferry with the magazine folded tightly into his *Business Review*.

What just happened here?

It was his custom to spend the thirty-five-minute ferry ride from the city reading the business newspapers or working, but today the *Business Review* stayed firmly folded, concealing its shameful secret. Conn had watched the newsagent pick up the magazine and fold it into his

paper, incredulous that the man would even *think* he would
buy a women's magazine. So incredulous that when
handed his purchases and change, he could only glare then
walk away, feeling ridiculous.

His embarrassment had faded into the occasional rueful
shake of the head by the time the ferry docked and he got
into his car and drove home. But it returned full force
when the object of his discomfort stood outside his door
with her hand on the doorbell. Con turned the engine off
and shoved the magazine into his briefcase before stepping
out of the car.

Annoyance mingled with intrigue. He did not like sur-
prises and considered he had wasted enough time thinking
about Ms. A-List Summers tonight. But there was no doubt
she interested him. Was that because she was famous?
Would he be as interested if she was a nobody?

A quick scan of her body confirmed that he would be.
More slender than she appeared on the television screen,
but still, she had curves that would turn any man's head.
And she walked as though she knew it. Denim-clad hips
swayed as her long legs started toward him and she raised
an elegant hand in greeting.

She looked a hundred percent better than their first
meeting. It was nearly dark, and his security light lit up the
driveway and picked out the shine of her hair. It was several
different shades, one of which clashed spectacularly with
her very pink sweater. And she must have found her makeup crew, because the face was just like it was in the cover
photo. Flawless skin. Practiced smile.

A warning flashed through his mind. Just remember, to
a newshound, there is no such thing as "off the record."

Then she stood in front of him, and his misgivings were

obliterated by a most pleasurable and searing rush of desire. It hit him low and hard and snatched away his breath.

Okay, it had been a while since his last sexual encounter, but he should be able to control his libido better than that. A fourteen-year-old should be able to control his libido better than that.

Conn thanked heaven for heavy cashmere overcoats.

"Howdy, neighbor," she said, with a bright but hesitant smile. She'd dropped her arm to her side, and her palm rubbed her hip, and it occurred to him she was a little nervous. Charming, he thought. Dangerous. Why would a woman who made a living out of meeting people and setting them at ease be nervous?

"Ms. Summers."

"Eve," she told him, rubbing her hip harder. "I thought we'd give this neighbor thing another try, without the medication this time."

Eve had felt fully recovered and excited about exploring her new surroundings, and so she'd decided to pay her neighbor a visit, partly to apologize for her lack of manners but also to see if he lived up to the intrigue. Not just his looks, though she'd had several tempting flashbacks featuring his face, but his reasons for wanting to buy her house.

His house was little more than five minutes' walk up a gentle incline. It had felt wonderful to stretch her legs after being laid low with flu for weeks.

His name may have escaped her but, standing in front of him now, she knew her memory hadn't done justice to such impressive shoulders. He was big. Eve was almost overwhelmed, not only by his size but a physical presence that seemed to invade her space, making her want to step back. Puzzled, she searched his inscrutable expression for a sign of welcome. "Um, it was kind of you to be concerned the other night."

He tilted his head to the side, watchful and silent.

Eve chewed her lip. "I'm sorry if I wasn't as friendly as I could have been."

"You weren't friendly at all," he murmured.

She picked at a seam on her jeans, not sure how to respond. People were generally happy to see her, to converse. She was not one to put any store on celebrity, but this level of detachment toward her was not customary. "O-kay. I apologize for the other night. Can we start again?"

He rubbed his jaw with large, well-tended fingers.

"I'm afraid I lost your card. I don't even know what to call you."

"Conn." He did not extend his hand. "Bannerman."

Once again, Eve thought she'd heard that name before.

"Great place you have here." She flicked her eyes over the house she had been admiring before he arrived. It was built on the edge of a cliff, far above the ferry terminal. One-storied, a long, low expanse of wood, concrete and glass in a sleek half-moon design. Glass dominated, as it should in this setting. She bet the views would be exceptional from every room.

"Would you like to come in?"

She turned back to him, remembering her manners. "I wouldn't like to impose."

He led her into the house through the garage. Eve felt eclipsed by the breadth and length of the hallway, and the way his head made it through the doorway with mere inches to spare. Big man, big house. They walked into a huge kitchen/dining/living area with wall-to-wall windows. The floor was polished timber, magnifying the feeling of space. Neutral colors and the clever use of partitioning walls and differing ceiling heights made it seem as if the areas were separated, but it was, in effect, one massive room. There were no lights on and did not appear to be any drapes or blinds.

Far across the harbor, the tall buildings and towers of the city sparkled, interspersed by patches of dark—hills and parks. The curve of the island was dotted with sparse lights from the tiny settlements that made up the five thousand residents. To the right stretched the inky sea and the darker shadows of the other Hauraki Gulf islands, jutting up like fists.

Conn Bannerman tossed his briefcase onto a ten-setting kauri table and began to unbutton his coat. "Would you like some coffee? Something stronger?" He moved to the cooking area and flicked a couple of lights on.

"Coffee's fine," Eve answered, still entranced by the view. "Can I help?"

He did not answer. She turned to watch him. His back was to her. The suit jacket had come off now, and he was rolling his shirtsleeves up strongly muscled forearms. "Did you build this house?"

He turned around holding two enormous coffee mugs and a percolator. He flicked her a brief nod, then filled the pot with water and measured coffee grounds.

"Are you a builder?" Eve leaned on the twenty-foot-long kitchen island and searched the shadows of his face. The light was behind him, but he had a chin Superman might covet.

"I'm in construction, yes."

In a flash, her mind clicked into recall. "CEO of Bannerman, Inc. You're the Bannerman Stadium guy."

"The Gulf Harbor Stadium guy," he corrected, setting milk, sugar and teaspoons on the marble-topped counter between them.

She recalled the euphoria that gripped the country when the International Rugby Board announced that New Zealand would host the next World Cup. The building of the stadium was a contentious issue but it wasn't something she had followed closely.

She would have if she'd known that the man bestowed with the responsibility of building that stadium was such a hunk. His profile was stern and strong and in perfect proportion to his muscular bulk. He would look wonderful on camera....

He seemed at home in his kitchen, his movements efficient and effortless. She bet he'd never drop a spoon or cup, the complete opposite of her.

Hmm. If he was efficiently at home in his kitchen, did that imply there was no Mrs. Bannerman lurking about?

"Shall we sit down?"

Eve lifted her mug with both hands. They moved to the big table. One end was covered in papers, files and a laptop. His keys sat in a striking blue-and-white-striped pottery fruit bowl alongside bananas, kiwifruit and tangelos. She was glad he wasn't phobic about neatness.

He saw her glance at the clutter. "I work from home a lot of the time. I have an office but I enjoy this room."

"I can see why."

They sipped in silence for a moment. It was deathly quiet. She fought an insane urge to cry "Hello!" and listen for the echo. Eve couldn't bear to be without the constant hum of TV or music. "You know, I think my whole house would fit in this one room."

Conn sipped his drink and looked at her with interest. "Have you thought about my offer?"

Eve toyed with the handle of her mug. "My mind was mush at the time. I didn't think you were serious."

"I was, most definitely." His eyes were on her face. Attentive. Sharp, even, and really a nice shade of green. She amended her previous impression of coolness. More apt to say *controlled. Unflappable.*

Unforgettable.

The song "Unforgettable" started up in her mind and she hummed it absently until she saw his blink of surprise and stopped. It was a stupid, if harmless, habit of hers that unsettled some people.

Conn recovered and looked at her expectantly. Eve glanced around the room and opened her arms wide. "Why would you want my house when you have this house?"

"Why would a *TV star* want to live on this side of the island?"

The emphasis on "TV star" somehow compelled her to feel defensive. Was it intentional?

Conn's eyes were still on her face. "I don't know if Baxter told you. I own all of the land here from the turnoff, except that one little piece your house is on."

Without taking her eyes off him, she murmured, "So, don't be greedy."

Conn raised his chin and pointed it at the window. Eve followed the line of his gaze—to her house. In the glow of her porch light, she caught the gleam of her white crushed-shell path. A rush of affection for her tumbledown house swelled her chest. Funny to think she had bonded so quickly with the rising damp, threadbare carpet and creaky floorboards.

She was smiling when she turned back to him, but that faded when she saw his resolute expression. With sudden clarity, she understood exactly his purpose. "You think my house spoils your view."

"If it was any other room, I could dismiss it," Conn said. "But not this room."

Eve frowned. Snippets of the conversation with the previous owner returned. Mr. Baxter had not liked his neighbor one little bit. He gleefully accepted her offer on the house, saying that at least Mr. High and Mighty up the hill wouldn't get his hands on it.

He wanted to pull down her house? "Not wanting to state the obvious, but my house has been there for sixty or seventy years."

Conn did not reply.

"If you didn't like the look of it," she continued, "why did you build this room so that you could see the house from here?"

He shrugged. "The old man couldn't live forever."

"He's not dead. He's in a rest home."

"I am aware of that, Ms. Summers. But it's academic now, isn't it?"

She ignored the use of her married name—again. "And everyone's got their price, right?"

His look sharpened. "What's yours?"

Under that intense green gaze, Eve struggled to hold her temper. His arrogance eroded all of the attraction she'd felt a few minutes ago.

Moving here had been about giving herself time to decide what the next chapter of her life would bring. She was twenty-eight years old, never a day out of work and now unemployed. Divorced. Childless. She knew without doubt that she needed to put down roots. Come to terms with her regrets, which all seemed to have caught up with her since her sacking. She was actually grateful that the crazy life of a TV presenter was no longer hers. It had never been the real Eve Drumm.

She would not be pushed.

"Mr. Bannerman…" She gave him what she hoped was a sweet smile.

"Conn," he said smoothly.

"I am sorry if the sight of my house is something you can't live with, but grown-ups learn they can't get everything they want all of the time."

"Grown-ups also learn the value of money, especially money they don't have to work for."

"I may be out of work right now but it's still not for sale," she said firmly. "I can't believe you want to pull down my little old house for something so—self-indulgent."

Conn leaned back, the barest hint of a smile compressing his lips. To her eyes, he looked thoroughly indulged.

"I can afford to be self-indulgent, *Eve*. Can you?"

"I have a bit to come and go on, thank you."

"Name your price."

Her temper stirred and stretched. "You can't afford it."

For the first time she saw anger flare in his eyes. Not much, carefully controlled, but he definitely had *not* learned that he couldn't get everything he wanted all of the time.

Her heart gave a thump, but it wasn't fear or even apprehension she felt facing him down. It was excitement, in its purest form. And it was very worrying. "I will be making improvements," she told him, tossing her head. "In the meantime, get some blinds." She drained her cup and stood. "Thank you for the coffee."

Her neighbor stood also, forcing her to look up. His eyes drilled into her face. "You didn't answer my question. Why is a big-shot TV star interested in living on this side of the island, anyway?"

Eve shot him a look of disdain and stalked to the door. This hadn't gone well at all. With her back still to him, she said quietly, "I am *not* a big TV star. I'm just a regular person who wants a bit of peace and quiet."

She looked over her shoulder. The physical distance between them strengthened her. The distance in his eyes depressed her. "I'm sorry to have disturbed you. I thought with the two of us being close neighbors and no one else for miles around—well, it would be nice to have someone to call on in an emergency, is all."

That square jaw rose and he glared down his long nose at her. "The trendy artists and café set in the village will welcome someone like you. Up here the natives are not so friendly." He paused ominously. "In the meantime, an emergency is acceptable. Discussing my open offer on your house is acceptable. Unannounced visits are not."

It took all of the willpower Eve possessed not to slam the door in his face. Striding down the hill in the dark, it occurred to her he hadn't even offered her a lift home. She wouldn't have accepted, anyway.

"Put him out of your mind," she muttered to herself. There were bigger, more important things to think about.

She had an election to disrupt and an old enemy to vanquish.

Two

Conn almost groaned aloud when he saw Eve sitting up front, chatting to the purser. He considered turning and walking off the ferry, but this was the last one of the night. It was now or the office couch.

He slipped warily into a seat at the back. The ferry was almost empty. With a bit of luck, he could get off before she saw him when they got to Waiheke. He stretched his long legs out, pulled his coat collar up around his ears and squeezed his eyes shut.

He knew he had been arrogant and the passage of a few days was not long enough to let him forget. She'd made an overture of friendship, and he had thrown it back at her. He could still see her lovely face streaked with embarrassment and something worse, as if her eyes were bruised. Had it been so long that he'd forgotten how to act around a woman?

Forgotten how to act around people, period. Conn

avoided interaction with people. Even his parents had nearly given up on him. They had been a happy family unit once. Now he was lucky to speak to them once a month.

It used to be so different.

He could hear Eve's voice the whole way. It was a nice voice, warm, lilting, bright with humor. He pried his eyes open occasionally to watch her. Her hair swung and her hands were never still. The purser had a smile a mile wide.

Finally they docked and Conn did not look back. Of course she would have seen him; there were only a handful of passengers. He got into his car, feeling like a heel, and watched her walk across the road to the taxi rank. The deserted taxi rank.

Damn.

He and Eve were the only people who lived up on the ridge far above the terminal. Being only thirty minutes by ferry to New Zealand's largest city, Waiheke Island was a popular place to reside—if you could afford it. In the summer, day-trippers and tourists tripled the population, and the many hotels, resorts and hostels were full.

But this was out of season and, except for the ferry commuters, the roads were deserted. There would only be one or two taxis operating at this time of night.

His hands clenched the wheel.

The very thought of driving another person froze his guts. Conn was comfortable enough driving himself—he had taught himself to be. Driving was necessary to living in the twenty-first century.

But the thought of anyone else in the car when he was at the wheel had him straightening and shrinking from an ice-cold trickle of sweat. Because of Rachel.

He breathed in deeply. He could do this. It wasn't like

he never drove anyone these days. But he generally liked to prepare himself. Give himself a pep talk beforehand.

He knew he could not drive past his new neighbor in the dark of a late-autumn night.

Easing the car into gear, he drove across the road, stopped, then leaned over and opened the passenger door.

Eve actually looked like she was going to refuse. She pursed her mouth, giving the empty streets a last look. Conn began to hope she would turn him down. But then she picked up his briefcase from the passenger seat and slid into the car.

"Nice of you."

He grunted, inhaling something tangy and lemony. They set off sedately. Conn forced himself to relax his knuckles so they would not whiten around the wheel. His knee began to ache. It always did in times of stress. The demolition of that knee in the accident had ruined his rugby-playing career, but that was a small price to pay for the taking of a life.

"Working late?" she asked eventually.

"Business dinner." The road was dark with dew. Conn hated wet roads. "Don't you have a car?" he asked curtly.

"It's in a garage in town. I thought I might get a scooter to have on the island."

"Not suitable for the gravel road on the ridge." In the silence that followed, he chided himself for sounding so abrupt.

Eve sighed and leaned her head on the rest.

The engine droned in Conn's ears. He thought about her talking and laughing with the purser just minutes ago.

"How's the job hunting going?" he asked, lifting one damp hand off the wheel to wipe over his thigh.

"I landed a job today, actually."

Conn flashed her a quick glance. She seemed more subdued than elated.

"It's part-time," she continued. "Only a few hours a week from home." She looked at him and her chin tilted up. "It shouldn't interfere with my renovations."

His lips compressed. If she was planning renovations, she was not thinking of moving.

She looked tired. He decided to cut her some slack and steer clear of the house subject. "What's the job?"

Her voice warmed. "Gossip columnist, would you believe? For the *New City*."

Conn snapped a look at her, incredulous. "*Gossip* columnist?"

"It should be fun." Now she sounded defensive.

"Perfect," Conn muttered, shaking his head in derision.

There was a long silence and then she sighed gustily. "What is it exactly that you don't like about me?"

That jolted him. He wondered what she'd do if he told her he liked her so much, he'd bought a women's magazine about her. "I don't know you well enough to have formed an opinion."

"What is it—my politics? My interviewing style?"

He liked her interviewing style, always had. He admired the way she put her subjects at ease, and he had never watched a show of hers that involved the badgering technique employed by so many others. She was enthusiastic and expressive, especially her hands; she used her hands constantly on TV.

A rabbit shot across the road in front of him. Adrenaline flooded his body. It took a superhuman effort not to swerve or pound at the brake pedal.

Conn focused on the road and his breathing. You can

do this, you *do* do it. Every muscle in his body vibrated with tension.

A minute dragged by. When his breathing had calmed, he cleared his throat. "I think you should know, Ms. Summers, I regard the whole media machine as a level below stepping in spit."

Her cheeks blew out in a little huff of exasperation, and she turned away to stare out the window. Conn knew he would feel bad later, but right now he was too tense to address it.

Finally they approached their turnoff and he swung the car onto the gravel road. His eyes pricked with relief at the sight of her dilapidated letterbox a few hundred meters away. He flexed his aching leg and eased off the gas, indicating he was about to turn into her driveway.

"Just here is fine."

The big car rolled to a halt opposite her house. Conn peeled his hands off the steering wheel. Inhaling, he laced his fingers together, pressed down and cracked each knuckle, one by one. He saw her grimace, but the flow of tension ebbing out of his extremities was exquisite.

She handed him his briefcase and held his gaze for a second. "Not friends, then," she murmured and turned to get out of the car. "But I do thank you for the lift. Good night, Mr. Bannerman."

Arrogant pig! Eve slammed her way inside the empty house and flicked the kitchen radio on. Some neighbor. Living in the city, you expected detachment and disinterest from neighbors. Here there were just the two of them for miles around.

She felt like a glass of wine for the first time since the

flu. Pouring a large glass, she wandered into the lounge and stabbed at the TV with the remote.

Why did Conn Bannerman hate her? He could barely bring himself to speak to her. To think she had found him attractive. She wandered into her second bedroom and booted the computer up. The attraction was certainly not mutual.

Wine was the nectar of the gods, she thought, sipping. She and James had been passionate about it. Had an enormous collection in London—she wondered what had become of it after she'd walked away.

After the miscarriage…

The phone rang. Frowning, she checked her watch. It was her friend Lesley, one of the reporters who worked— had worked—on her show.

Eve's mood perked up. If she was going to be the *New City* newspaper's gossip columnist, there was no one better than Lesley to know what was going on in town. "How are you bearing up, Les?"

The very worst thing about being fired was that it affected all the people working on her show.

"I'm fine, Evie. Don't worry about me. There's plenty of work around. How's life in the slow lane?"

While she chatted with Lesley, Eve came across the card Conn had given her the other night. She typed in his company Web site. Waiting for the screen to come up, she asked her friend if she'd heard of Conn Bannerman.

"'Ice' Bannerman? The guy building the stadium?"

"They call him 'Ice'?" Eve asked, thinking how apt that was.

"Fearless on the field. Used to play rugby for New Zealand."

Eve raised her brows. That explained the killer bod.

New Zealand was a small country on the world stage but punched well above their weight in rugby. And they treated members of their national team like kings. Even past members. "Why haven't I heard of him?"

"Long time ago. Ten, eleven years."

"Ah, I was on the big OE." Overseas, backpacking around, producing the news in far-flung places. "Anything personal?"

"Hmm. I don't think he does interviews."

I sort of got that, Eve thought.

"Self-made millionaire. I think there was something—an accident, finished his playing career before it really took off. I'm not sure. But Jeff will know. I'll get him to look it up." Lesley's boyfriend was a sports editor.

"Now listen up. Have you checked your e-mails? Your mystery contact called today."

Eve banged her glass down, slopping wine in her rush to sign into her e-mail.

"He's sent you a teaser," Lesley continued. "A couple of photos. They say a picture tells a thousand words."

Eve flopped back in her seat, staring at the monitor.

The photos were poor quality, grainy and unfocused. It wasn't the skimpily clad, almost prepubescent girls that widened Eve's eyes. Nor the opulence of the yacht the subjects were on. It was the three middle-aged men the girls were draped over that had her scrambling for a pen and scribbling frantically on her deskpad.

Three well-known names.

One, a businessmen who was at the very top tier of big business. The second man was the current police commissioner. The third—she groaned in disgust—was on the board of the government-owned television network. The one she'd worked for.

"What else? Did he say anything else?"

"He asked for your phone number—I told him you would have to agree to that. I guess he'll be in touch. And he wants you to know he's sorry if you got sacked on his account."

Eve frowned. How did he know she was sacked? The official word was she'd quit.

"Oh, and he said to tell you it's not always about money."

Eve pondered that. How did this relate to Pete Scanlon?

She hadn't seen her nemesis since she was fifteen. It had been a huge shock to her when he'd burst onto the political scene here six months ago. No one knew anything about him. He was progressive and personable. He was handsome and articulate. People said he was vibrant.

Eve had invited him on the show but he declined, knowing full well she detested him. She made the comment on air that perhaps the show should go to his home town down south—her home town—and find out what his peers thought, since he chose to be so elusive.

Then an anonymous businessman called her at the studio, claiming Pete's tax consultancy had involved him and other prominent businessmen in shady deals amounting to tax evasion. While trying to persuade him to name names publicly, Eve proposed exploring the issue in a segment on the show. Her boss said no which had led to a huge row and Eve being fired.

Then she'd gotten sick, moved and succumbed to a relapse.

Now Pete Scanlon was set to shake this city of one and a half million on its head. So much more scope for damage than a few country bumpkins. Eve intended to make sure the people of her adopted city knew what they were getting before they cast their votes.

"You really have it in for this guy, don't you?" her friend asked.

Eve took a large sip of wine and swirled it around her mouth to dilute the bad taste the thought of that man always left. "You know that old adage about a leopard changing its spots? That will never happen to Pete Scanlon. He is bad, through and through."

Lesley promised to pass on her phone number when the contact called again. Eve stared at the photos on the screen for minutes after hanging up, wondering what they meant.

It's not always about money.

What did an opulent yacht, some underage girls and two out of the three men working for the government have in common with dodgy tax deals?

Only that Pete Scanlon was involved. The lightbulb went on. Blackmail and corruption, so much more his style than business.

Praying her mystery man would contact her again soon, she considered her options. The only weapon at her disposal now was the gossip column. First thing tomorrow she would contact the legal team at the paper. Her words would have to be very carefully chosen to avoid slam-dunking the fledgling paper into a defamation war.

Eve signed out, her mood grim, but her path ahead was clear. Stop Pete Scanlon.

Her eye was drawn to the business card of the CEO of Bannerman, Inc. For the second time, she crumpled the card in her hand and tossed it on the floor.

And told herself to stop thinking about Conn Bannerman!

Three

Conn paused by his secretary's desk. "Phyll, do you read the *New City?*"

His secretary looked surprised. "No, Mr. Bannerman."

He carried on into his office. As he removed his jacket, Phyllis followed him in, held out a wad of messages and took his coat from him in the same movement. "I think I saw one in the tearoom."

Conn looked at her blankly.

"The newspaper. Shall I get it?"

"Thank you."

To anyone who did not know her, his secretary looked unperturbed. Conn, however, knew the level of astonishment she displayed in her arched brows and pursed lips. He read only the business papers. The *New City* was hardly what one would call a serious newspaper, chock-full as it was of entertainment news and fashion.

Eve Summers invaded his mind for the umpteenth time today, as she had every day since their last meeting. He had seen her once since giving her a lift home. She'd been chopping wood into kindling in the lopsided lean-to she used as a wood shed. She hadn't turned and waved as he drove past. He had not expected her to.

He could hardly be blamed for being so unpleasant the other night. If she only knew what it cost him to drive her.

Phyllis tapped on the door and entered the room, placing the newspaper on the corner of his desk. Conn pretended to concentrate on his work. He bet Phyll would know how to make amends to a minor acquaintance she had slighted.

He bet Phyll would have a coronary if he asked her.

Alone again, he reached out for the folded paper and noted the small advertising box on the front page: Our New Gossip Columnist, Perennially Popular EVE DRUMM! (formerly SUMMERS!)

How could she stoop so low? Conn's lip curled. She'd described the position as fun. People's embarrassments and misfortunes all thrown into the pot, mixed well and served up as fun?

He tossed the paper back on the desk and bent his head to his work.

After a hectic day, Conn settled on the ferry and finally opened the *New City* newspaper. He proceeded to read the thing from cover to cover, leaving her column till last. It was almost like postponing his reward.

That was his mistake. Had he read her column first, the flash of temper it inspired would have had longer to cool by the time he drove up Eve's driveway. Conn may have taken a moment to wonder whether the article itself angered him or it was just an excuse to see her again.

"Damn it all!" he muttered, throwing the car into park. He strode up her pathway as if he could outrun the steam coming out of his ears. It was bad enough that there was a celebrity living next door. He'd already heard music on the night air a couple of times. The glitzy parties were bound to start anytime. There would be cars cluttering up the roads and fancy caterers' vans and no doubt photographers hiding in the bushes.

But the fact that she was also a gossip columnist—the lowest of the low—only added to his ire.

She opened the door to his loud knocking, a startled look on her face. Conn did not wait for an invitation. He brushed past her, saluting her with the paper. After several moments she closed the door and followed him into the kitchen.

Conn slapped the paper down on top of the table while she moved to switch off the radio on the bench. It didn't make any difference; there was still music blaring.

"You've gone too far," he told her loudly.

Frowning, Eve turned to the window and pulled the curtain back. She wore the same pink sweater as the other night and black pants. Very slinky black pants, the kind with no zip in front.

"What are you doing?" he demanded of her shapely hip as she peered out into the twilight.

"The thunder clap's arrived," she said drily. "Where's the lightning?" She let the curtain fall and turned back, leaning her hip against the bench.

Conn stared at her, biting the inside of his lip to stop himself from smiling. Damn it! He raised the folded newspaper and gave it a loud flick. "You'll be laughing on the other side of your face when my legal team is through with you."

"Oh, the column." Her face cleared and she fluttered her

fingers at the paper he held. "Funny. I didn't pick you as a fan of gossip columns."

"I'm not!" he snapped. "It was—brought to my attention."

A wariness sharpened her gaze. "What's he to you?"

Conn raised his tense shoulders. "For your information, my company is backing Pete Scanlon to the hilt in the mayoralty campaign."

That seemed to jolt her. Two little lines appeared between her wide-set indigo eyes. "You mean financially?"

"Yes, financially. What else?" How she stirred him up! Every reaction he had around this woman was extreme. There were no nice soft corners. It was all slashes of anger, of suspicion, of confusion.

Of desire.

"Are you close?"

Conn snorted. "What do you mean, close? I give him money for his election campaign. I do that because I need him to win. I need him to win so I can do my job."

There was some hideous piece of opera playing in the next room. He could hardly hear himself think. Eve leaned three feet away, her chin jutting out in defiance. Once again, he had put her on the defensive by being insufferable.

"So you don't socialize with him?"

"I hardly know the man," Conn told her impatiently. Surely she'd noticed he was not the type to socialize. "But I won't have him slandered in rags like this."

Eve lifted her shoulders and placed both palms on her chest. "*My* legal team went through it with a fine-tooth comb. You won't find a word in there you can do anything about."

Conn struggled to keep his eyes on her face and not the indentations her fingers made, pressing in on her front. "You know what I think? You made it up."

"Think so?" she taunted softly. Either she had lowered her voice or the music was getting louder. Her eyes were wide and teasing. Her mouth, half smiling, baited him. All he could think was would she still be smiling after he kissed her?

"Can we turn that blasted racket off?" he barked.

That wiped the complacent look off her face. She threw her arms up in the air and stalked into the lounge. He was one step behind her as she swerved to avoid a cluster of sanding gear, masks and tins of paint stripper on the bare floor.

"Your attempt to discredit Scanlon is a publicity stunt. Admit it."

She stopped in front of the stereo and whirled on him. "No, it's gossip. You know, a lighthearted dig about how pleased his former subjects are that he's moved on to bigger and better pastures."

When she didn't move, Conn reached over her shoulder, his finger jabbing at the stereo power switch. The opera was cut off midaria but the television set in the corner of the room was still chattering. "Your career is over and you can't accept that because you have an insatiable need to be in the public eye. Because you people make up things to draw attention to yourselves." He could not believe how heightened his senses were, how his blood seemed to surge through his veins.

"I do not!" she retorted, not backing up one inch.

"Why then, *Ms.* Summers…" He leaned in close. Since his finger already had its dander up, he employed it to wag in front of her astonished face. "Why are there no names? No confirmations? But mostly, why is yours the lone voice in the wilderness?"

She grabbed his finger.

He started, unable to believe it. A jolt of energy crackled and popped through him at the contact. Yes, she had a tight hold on his index finger and was holding it away, so there was nothing in between them.

Nothing but air and madness.

In a flash his big hand totally encompassed her small one and he laced their fingers together.

She tossed her head back, inhaling sharply. "Because, *Mr.* Bannerman," she said, dragging her incredulous eyes from their entwined fingers to his face, "Scanlon cultivates friends in high places. He always has."

Conn moved a step closer, tugging her hand gently toward him. "Really, *Ms.* Summers?"

"The New City paper isn't part of the old-boy network. It…it can't be bought off like the others." Her breathing seemed shallow and rapid, her voice not as certain as before. But she did raise her chin. "And it's *Drumm,* not Summers."

Their wrists had locked together and he felt her pulse hammering against his. "Sorry. Ms. *Drumm.*" He bowed his head mockingly. "A rag's a rag. Pete Scanlon has probably never even heard of it." There was no heat in his voice now, the anger dissipating with the feel of her unresisting hand in his. Unresisting but not unresponsive. When he saw her eyes flick to his mouth and away, his blood began pumping to another beat. It wasn't opera.

"I bet he has now," she murmured and something glowed in him to hear her breathlessness.

Conn brought his other hand up and took her free one. She sucked in a breath but her warm fingers closed around his and her eyes flicked back and stayed on his mouth. He moved closer, dipping his head.

"Conn?" she breathed. Her eyes were wide and dark, her chest rose as his body connected with hers.

"Eve." He took her mouth. Soft and cool and firm. His anger and tension fell away. Sighing, he pulled her closer. This was the argument he had wanted to have with her since day one.

She made a little humming noise in her throat and flexed her hands, but he wasn't giving them up just yet. He eased her arms behind her and placed their laced hands on her rump. They swayed together, mouths locked, pressing up against each other.

He touched his tongue to hers, and exhilaration fizzed through him—that she tasted like heaven, that she was compliant, that maybe she was as greedy as he was.

Conn was so hungry for this warmth, this need, her acceptance. He was no monk, but it had been a long time. His infrequent affairs were more like arrangements, begun with the objective of completion. There wasn't this blind need reaching out from him, building out of all proportion to the situation. Right out of proportion for a first kiss for two people who couldn't even decide if they trusted or liked each other.

He leaned over her a little and angled her head back so he could kiss her more deeply. His desire built relentlessly and it flowed like tendrils of silk, binding them closer. He felt her slim fingers tightening rhythmically around his and her hips swaying as she arched against him. She was leading him into madness, and he'd never been more willing in his life.

When her tongue slid against his, the room began to swirl and he knew he'd reached his point of no return. She was leading him somewhere he might not be able to leave.

They came apart slowly, watching each other. Conn's mouth tingled and his body ached with desire, and he felt that it would for the rest of the night. Eve looked into his eyes as if she had never seen him before.

He slowly leaned back, bringing their still-joined hands to her front. Her tight grip relaxed but she did not pull away.

He took a deep breath, inhaling that tangy citrus lotion or shampoo or whatever it was she wore. "I'm—sorry. That was not meant to happen."

Her head jerked. Big eyes, as big as his, no doubt.

He released her hands with one last gentle squeeze. "I think I made my point," he said, with little certainty. Then he nodded and walked out to his car.

Eve was a pacer. When alone and troubled, she would pace while conversing out loud, throwing her arms around to accentuate her points. But minutes after the sound of Conn's car faded away, she stood exactly where he'd left her.

The initial clamoring of desire, from scalp to toes, was fading, too—into worry. She didn't want to regret this kiss. Why should she regret something that warmed her through, reminded her of the joy of being a woman? She loved that stomach-plummeting feeling, like dreaming you're falling off a cliff—scary but not fatal. Her blood was pumping and, yes, her juices flowed and it felt fantastic.

But this was a path already trodden. Eve did not trust lust. It had led directly to her marriage. In fact, if you wanted to think about it, her ex-husband's lust—for other women—had led directly to her divorce.

Oh, no. She could not, she would not be drawn again into a relationship based on the physical.

"Don't trust lust." That would be her mantra. That night,

she recited it until she fell asleep, and again when she woke up. Eve made a firm resolution to stay away from Conn Bannerman unless—unless her house was on fire.

Wouldn't he just love that? she thought wryly.

The next day she received a small packet of newspaper clippings about Conn's past from Lesley's boyfriend. Not yet she thought, tossing it unopened in a kitchen drawer. Not with the taste of his kiss still fresh in her memory.

She spent the next few days following leads on Pete Scanlon. In a worrying turn of events she discovered that her ex-boss, Grant, was also thick with the mayoral candidate. She'd been fond of Grant. There was a kindliness in him unusual in the cutthroat world of TV ratings. She suspected sacking her had been difficult for him and he'd certainly copped a lot of public flak since her departure.

However, for Pete Scanlon to be friendly with two leading personnel of the national TV station put a sinister slant on Eve's exit from that station.

A call from the mystery businessman gave her insight into a surprisingly clever money laundering and tax scam. Eve was surprised. The Pete Scanlon she knew was boorish and unrefined. Yet he had devised a simple but effective way to exploit the gray area between tax avoidance and tax evasion.

But then her contact moved onto the blackmail part of it, and that involved not only the businessmen he had already compromised but also government and police officials, politicians, media moguls. Private yacht trips, everything supplied—drugs, girls, gambling, whatever took their fancy. And, of course, the hidden camera.

"It's not money that spins Pete's wheels," the man told her. "It's power. Turn the screws and keep the favors coming. Forever."

Oh, yes, this was so much more his style.

"Will you go on record?" Eve implored, without much hope. The stakes were far higher than she'd realized.

"Not on my own," the man said. "If this all comes out, a couple of the players could get jail time. Others—and I'm in that category—will get massive fines and destroyed reputations."

"He will win this election," Eve fretted, her faith in the incumbent mayor dwindling. "Benson's stale. The people want something new."

"You have around three weeks to do something about it. Else there won't be a clean cop or politician or newsman in this city."

Eve was jarred by the sudden realization that Conn could be of the business cartel involved in the money laundering. Or worse, what if the not-so-honorable mayoral candidate had something awful hanging over his head?

The packet of clippings had taunted her for two days. Her resolution to stay away from him was strong. But if her neighbor was implicated in Pete's web of deceit, best she be prepared.

Her hand trembled as she slit open the plastic envelope. Conn's past, all rubber-banded in chronological order, fell out.

The car's tires crunched to a halt in her driveway. "Check one," Eve muttered and stood up from the couch, smoothing her top.

A car door slammed. "Check two." She picked up the full wineglass from the mantel where it had been warming.

Determined footfalls pulverized her shell footpath. "Check three," she whispered, and her heartbeats thumped in tandem with her steps down the hall toward her door.

Bang! Bang! Bang! "Check four," she said under her breath, and turned the lock.

The thunderous glower. *Check five.* She smiled serenely and offered him the glass.

Conn gaped. What started as a terrific frown slowly smoothed out into confusion. His eyes moved from her face to the glass and back.

"Come in. It's cold." Eve stepped closer, holding out the glass, and he had no option but to take it. She ushered him in and closed the door. "Come down to the lounge. The fire's going." She turned and walked down the hallway.

Doing her best to appear unperturbed, she poked the fire, then picked up her glass off the mantel and sipped the brackish red liquid. It was a full twenty, nail-biting seconds to the beat of an old Pink Floyd song, before Conn appeared. He stood, dwarfing the doorway, looking at her.

She took another big sip and let it rest in her mouth for a few moments while she submitted to the rake of his eyes. She had taken care dressing and was comfortable under his scrutiny, even if her pulse thumped in her ears.

After a long perusal, Conn raised his glass and sipped. "Is the wine okay?"

He swallowed and inclined his head.

She carefully let her breath out and watched while he did a leisurely circle of the room. He reminded her of a wild animal, marking his territory. He paused often, studying every object: her four-foot wooden tiger, the burnished, naked art torso on the wall that seemed to move in the flickering firelight, a couple of family photos. Once his hand reached out to smooth over a section of wall that she had stripped and sanded for painting. He glanced at the candles on the coffee table and again at the line of tea lights on the mantel. He stared for quite a few moments at the platter of cheese and olives and dipping oils for the little chunks of crusty bread.

Eve inhaled. If he was going to lose it, it would be now.

Not once did he glance her way until he had come full circle. Then he stopped by the couch, brows raised sardonically in a pretence of asking her permission to sit.

Eve nodded.

When he was seated, he took another sip of wine, then leaned forward and placed the glass on the coffee table.

"You've gone to a lot of trouble." He pointed his chin at the glass. "Wine. Food. Candles." He looked up at her standing in front of the fire. *You.* The unspoken word danced in his eyes as they flickered and glowed up and down her body like the reflected flames.

"It was nothing." Eve stilled the fluttering hand that betrayed her nerves.

He tilted his head. "Your column."

She nodded. Her second column was a surefire way to get his attention. Not that that was her sole motivation, but someone had to make the move. It was five days since the kiss. Reasonable people could not storm into her house, roar at her, kiss her silly and then ignore her.

So much for resolutions....

Conn frowned and leaned back with his hands behind his head. "This isn't just small-town gossip, Eve. It's serious now."

"It *is* serious."

"Money laundering. Blackmail. You cannot go around making up these things without any proof."

"I'm confident," Eve said, "that I will be backed up." Fairly confident, she amended silently.

"The election is less than three weeks away," Conn was saying. "Are you planning on being 'backed up' before then, or is this just your common smear campaign?"

Eve knelt on the floor and rested her arms on the coffee table. "Can I ask you a couple of questions about your relationship with Pete?" She held up her hand when he frowned and began to speak. "Don't explode on me. Just answer me honestly. It's important."

Conn bowed his head.

His face suited firelight as much as it would a camera. "One—are you doing any business, specifically off-shore business with Pete Scanlon or his tax consultancy? Two— is he declaring your campaign contributions?" Again, she raised her hand against the toss of his head. "Three…hear me out, Conn. Is he blackmailing you?"

The Pink Floyd CD had finished and the next CD was loud rock. She saw him grimace but stayed where she was, wanting to watch his face when he answered.

"No, I presume so, and no." His voice was unequivocal and loud, his eyes unwavering.

Oh, thank God. She hadn't realized how badly she needed to hear that. To believe that he was noble and honest and had arrived at his level of success with his integrity intact. Because now there wasn't just her house and that kiss and the matter of Pete Scanlon between them. Now she knew his darkest secrets. His past had touched her heart.

Conn was still frowning. "Why don't you sit up here—" he patted the couch beside him "—and tell me just what your beef is."

"Okay." She started to rise.

"But first," Conn halted her, "do we have to listen to *that?*" He tilted his head sharply at the stereo.

Eve grinned and got to her feet. "I like music."

"If that's what passes for music these days, I'm glad I don't bother. And did you know your kitchen radio is blaring?"

She selected an easy-listening compilation and turned the volume down. Scooping up her glass, she made herself comfortable on the end of the couch with her legs drawn up under her. "Sorry. Habit." She took a noisy slurp of wine and pushed the platter of food toward him. "My parents were profoundly deaf."

Conn looked up from the platter, a stunned expression on his face.

Eve smiled, fond memories filling her mind. "Mum used to go around the house before I got home from school and turn every radio, stereo, TV on, full bore. She didn't want me to feel I was growing up in a silent house." Laughter bubbled up in her throat. "And Dad used to dance with me. We would dance all over the house, trying to drag my poor mother into it."

The olive in his hand was still midway to his mouth.

"Don't worry," she laughed. "Deafness didn't hold them back any. Or me."

"You're not…"

She shook her head. "It wasn't genetic. Dad's mother had rubella when she was pregnant. Mum got meningitis when she was three months old."

"I thought your father…"

The good memories faded. She blinked at the fire. "He passed away just over a year ago." To cover the awful hollow feeling in her chest, Eve leaned forward and dipped some bread in oil. "Mum still lives in Mackay, down south."

For a long time she could not think of her beloved father without sobbing. Since being fired, she was slowly coming to terms with the pain and injustice of losing him so early. It was to her everlasting shame that she had taken exactly one day off work when he died.

That was what she did—used to do—throw herself into work to push away her regrets. But they all caught up with her a few short weeks ago and she was done running.

"Can you sign?"

Startled from her reverie, Eve dropped the bread she was holding on to the coffee table. Conn moved fast and mopped up with a paper napkin.

"Thanks. That's another legacy of growing up with deaf parents. I am extremely clumsy. Comes from signing in a hurry. Like when Mum's about to step on the cat's tail. You just drop everything and sign." She raised her hands and signed *Stop!*

Conn leaned back on the arm of the couch and faced her with a broad smile.

Her heart slid inside her chest and she sucked in and held her breath. It was the first smile she had ever seen on his handsome face. It held the promise and warmth of the best sunrise ever. Eve could have looked at him all night, just sitting across from her, smiling.

Four

Conn was uncomfortably aware too-tight skin stretched over cheekbones stretched in an uncustomary smile; his appreciation of the way the fire glow burnished her skin, singed her pale-toffee hair and danced in her eyes, was a good enough reason to get up and walk right now. *You grinning fool!*

She made him uneasy, acutely aware of her, or at least of his response to her. What was it to him if she had deaf parents, a taxing childhood? Everyone had their problems. Right now his job was to convince her to cease her war on the mayor-to-be, not to remember how she felt in his arms.

Conn licked suddenly dry lips and recalled the texture and taste of her mouth on his. Exasperated, he glanced around the room.

Eve Drumm was dangerous. He had been set up for seduction with her candles and firelight and wine. She'd been expecting him. She wore a sheer, flowing tunic top in muted golden colors over soft dark pants—hardly the attire of a woman home alone. Diamonds twinkled at her ears. Her makeup was perfect. The wine was expensive.

He should be—he was—flattered, but it bothered him that she had lured him here.

He *still* wanted to kiss her.

With a quick shake of his head, he leaned forward and snagged himself some bread. "What was it like having two deaf parents?"

Eve launched into her tale with a bright smile, the constant motion of her hands drawing his eye. He understood better now the humming, the expressive hands.

"It was a great childhood in the early days." Small town, everyone knew each other. Her parents were close and worked hard to ensure she did not miss out on anything. "I got the usual ribbing at school about having deaf parents, but it was nothing I couldn't handle. That's the way they brought me up."

Her father was an internationally acclaimed designer of hearing implant modifications, she told him with pride. It was fastidious work, requiring great concentration, but it meant they lived well and her mother could afford to be a stay-at-home mum.

Conn marveled at the way emotion played over her features, illuminating her face with bright affection, shadowing it with sadness.

"In a small town, there is always someone with a lot of power, more important than anyone else. That person in Mackay was Pete's father. He was a judge. He had everyone in his pocket. His son got away with everything. There were never any consequences for Pete, but always plenty for everyone else."

Her glass was nearly empty and Conn rose and brought the bottle from the mantel. He topped up their glasses and settled back on the couch.

"I was eleven," she continued, staring into the fire. "Pete's maybe ten years older than me. He had a hot car. He and his boy racer mates used to spend every Friday and Saturday nights spreading diesel across the roads and racing their cars. There had been several accidents, but the police wouldn't touch him because of his father's influence."

She explained how her father had been driving home one wet night and had the misfortune to drive over the exact spot where the boy racers had been a few minutes earlier. He was not able to control the skid and ploughed headlong into a tree. "He was lucky to survive," she told him quietly. "He had a punctured lung and his right hand was terribly mangled. He also fractured his skull and suffered a brain injury. Everything changed after that."

Conn leaned back, hardly breathing. He knew how a split second could rip the seat out of someone's world.

"Dad recovered quite well but his brain injury meant he could no longer concentrate long enough to do his job. He couldn't have, even without the brain injury, because of his poor hand. He became morose and moody. The laughter was gone. He hated that he couldn't support us like before."

Where was the shallow celebrity now? Conn wondered. Admiration for her resilience rose in him.

"Things got worse. No way did he want to become a charity case. He tried to find work, but his age, his deafness, his disabled hand…he was reduced to sweeping the floors at the local freezing works." Now sorrow was etched into her face. "My brilliant, happy, loving father, reduced to menial labor."

Conn nodded with heartfelt sympathy. He too knew what it was like to watch the love for life bleed out of a father's face. The difference was, in his father's case, *he* had been responsible.

"With his medical bills and less money coming in, things were pretty tough. When I hit my teens, naturally I wanted the same stuff my friends did—music, clothes, makeup—but there wasn't enough to go around. I started babysitting. Scanlon was married by then with a toddler. One night I babysat for them. Dad would have hit the roof if he'd known. Anyway, Pete insisted on driving me home even though he'd been drinking. He tried to grope me. His hands were all over me." Eve shuddered. "He reeked of scotch whiskey. The smell of it still turns my stomach."

Conn realized that the scraping noise he could hear was the sound of his own teeth grinding.

"I was more than a match for him, but I couldn't say anything because my parents would have been gutted to know I'd babysat for him." She sighed heavily. "And so, once again, he had won. He had gotten away with it."

Eve fell silent then while Conn struggled with his anger. The thought of Scanlon's hands on her. It did not take too much imagination to conjure up her youthful fear and disgust. It made him want to punch something.

Which was dumb. He didn't have the right to be jealous. He certainly did not *want* the right to be jealous. His motive in coming here was to derail her smear campaign. No matter what he thought of Pete Scanlon, he needed him.

So he nodded and fixed her with a sympathetic gaze. "I'm sorry."

Eve shrugged. "A drunken grope is the least of his crimes."

"When did you last see him?"

"That was the last time."

"Maybe he's changed."

She snorted. "Yeah, right! Three or four years ago, just before I came home from the UK, he won the mayoralty of Mackay. The election was rigged. Nobody in the town liked him, quite the opposite. He and his father's bully-boy tactics won the day. His first official duty was to close the freezing works, which put thirty percent of the town's population out of work."

"Including your father." Some pretty valid justification there, he conceded. "I'm sorry for what you went through, and I can understand how you feel. But it's ancient history, Eve. You're letting your personal dislike of the man color your judgment."

Eve's eyes flashed. "Did you not read my column? I may be just a gossip columnist to you, Conn, but I cut my teeth on producing the news. I know where there's meat in a story. I know corruption when I smell it."

Conn gently swirled the liquid around in his glass. "This city needs a change. The present climate is intolerable for business. Especially my business."

"But the man is morally bankrupt!"

The passion in her voice surprised him. Her hands stabbed the air. Her eyes blazed. It was enviable, her assumption that it was okay to express emotion. He was so used to keeping everything in.

He was more comfortable that way.

"Look, I couldn't care less about him personally but to be honest, I can't afford him not to win. The present regime is stalling my stadium."

"But there's loads of public support for the stadium," Eve protested.

"But not the mayor's support and therefore not the council's support. I'm waiting months for consents and inspections that are usually done in days."

"And Scanlon's promised to smooth the way, right? That's what he does. He promises you the world, but you can bet he'll want favors in return."

"He's getting favors. He's getting money for his campaign."

"I'm sorry but I have to play my hand. The people deserve to know what they're getting. He's a big fish in a bigger pond here. His father can't protect him."

Conn set his glass down, tiring of the argument. "There are wider issues to consider."

Her eyes darkened with warning. "Distance yourself, Conn. My source is naming names. When he goes down— and he will—he will take others with him."

"You seem very sure of that."

With a hiss, a log rolled out of the fire onto the hearth. Conn moved quickly, jabbing at it with the poker. Eve grabbed the hearth brush, crouching to swipe at the embers sparkling on her rug. Her tangy scent drifted up through the wood smoke and candle wax to where he stood.

Brushing the last ember back into the fire, she looked up and grinned. "Thanks."

Her smile faded as he stared at her for an indecently long time. The logs shifted uneasily in the grate, sending another shower of sparks up the chimney like the blood fizzing through his veins. The heat from the fire enveloped them in a fierce glow of yearning. Danger, he thought again. She made him want what he couldn't have. But it was best they stay on opposite sides of the fence, politically and physically.

"That fireplace needs some serious remedial work," he told her.

Eve rolled her eyes. "Doesn't everything? The more I strip back, the worse it gets."

"I could send in a few men to give you a hand. There are enough of my men sitting on their backsides doing nothing while we're waiting on the council."

She put out a hand and laid it on his forearm, exerting a slight pressure to pull herself up. That teasing look was back. He remembered it from last time. The look that said, "Try me. I dare you."

"Does this mean you're not intent on running me out of town, neighbor?"

They were less than a foot apart. He curled his fingers into his palms to stop himself from plunging them into her soft hair. "I'm calling a truce, till I decide what to do about this insane urge I have to kiss you all the time."

She ghosted closer, her hand tightening on his arm. Appreciation of his honest statement shone in her eyes, and the warning bells began to clang. He drew himself up, flicking a glance around the room. Candles, wine, the slinky flowing outfit that begged to be slipped down her shoulders. Him cornered in *her* corner of the jungle.

She opened her mouth, and her voice was a silken invitation. "Is that so insane?"

Conn came out of his corner swinging. In one smooth movement, his hands cupped her face, tilted it up, and he crushed his lips down on hers. It was shockingly brief and hard. His eyes were open, scowling. But what started out as a lesson in not pushing threatened to lose its shape and purpose. For a microsecond he could not resist just a touch of tenderness.

But he closed down that idea with ruthless determination and jerked his head up, still holding her face firmly in both hands.

Satisfaction leaped in him when confusion and then understanding dawned in her eyes. She learned fast.

"When—if—I decide to kiss you," he growled, "it'll be on *my* terms. *I'll* do the running."

Conn resisted the urge to soothe the cord of tension in her neck and let his hands drop instead. "Be very careful, Eve."

The warning had nothing to do with her smear campaign.

Where was she? he wondered, days later.

He walked from her closed front door and stood at her gate, glaring down the road as if that would make her materialize. Then he turned his glare on the letterbox, the real reason for his animosity.

Stone, carved so it looked like woven flax. It was a Jordache, one of the more prominent artists and sculptors who lived on the island. Conn just happened to walk past his studio and there it was and he thought of Eve. He knew she liked Jordache; he'd noticed a small piece on the chest in her lounge. He'd paid the man, arranged for the installation and then waited for her call of thanks.

The call didn't come. Perhaps she had so many admirers she hadn't realized the expensive sculpture was a housewarming gift from her neighbor. He considered calling her but with her being a celebrity, she would be unlisted.

Her lights weren't on the next night, either. There was no acrid wood smoke polluting the pristine island air. None of her music irritating the omnipresent murmur of sea and wind and nature. He prowled his house, restless and strangely unappreciative of his treasured silence. He had the best music system money could buy piped throughout the house—but no CDs. The radio stations were intrusive but he did find a half-decent classical station.

Finally, four days after the letterbox had arrived, she deigned to give him a call.

"Do you have anything to do with that fabulous work of art at my gate?"

Telling himself he was irritated, Conn nearly denied all knowledge. Eve raced on in her animated style, and he rose from his table and turned off the radio so he could hear her voice unhindered. By the time she paused for breath, he was smiling to himself, even while wondering why.

"I *love* Jordache," she enthused. "Did you notice I had a piece? Of course, I could only afford the smallest thing he ever made. How can I accept it?"

Conn put on his best scowl. "It's set in concrete," he gruffed. "Besides, your mail box was a disgrace."

"It was, wasn't it? Oh, Conn, it's the best present I ever had. How can I ever thank you? You'll come to dinner!" Her excited chatter stopped abruptly. "Oh, sorry," she said more sedately. "I'm being pushy again."

Conn's rolled his head back, recalling his words about doing the running.

The brief silence did not seem to faze her. She prattled on about how busy she'd been, doing the rounds of parties and coffee meetings with friends and staying in town. All grist for her column, naturally. And how she had finished preparing the walls in the house and had been on a paint-buying spree.

So when Sunday arrived he gave up his pretence at

working and walked down the hill to her house. The bronze hatch of the letterbox glinted in the morning sun. Eve answered the door wearing paint-splattered overalls over a melon-colored long-sleeved tee. She looked about twelve years old, and Conn struggled not to return her smile of greeting.

"I've got a couple of hours free," he announced. "I could give you a hand with the painting."

Her mouth dropped open.

"I have painted before," he told her curtly.

"Yes. It's just, um…no, that's fine. That's great. It seems to be taking forever." She led him inside, looking him up and down over her shoulder. "I have overalls but none that would fit you, I'm afraid."

"I'll have to be careful then, won't I?"

She stopped at the second door down the hall. "Um, in here."

He understood her hesitation when he found himself in her bedroom. It was small, most of the space taken up by a very large bed. The double walk-in wardrobe doors were mirrors. There was no other furniture save one bedside table and the bench seat under the bay window, both draped in sheeting. Another door led through to the attached bathroom.

Because the wardrobe was large and the room small, it seemed everywhere he looked, he could see both of them and the hulking shape of the bed in the mirrors.

"Nice colors," he muttered, wondering what the hell he was doing here. Of all the rooms in her house, why did she have to be painting her bedroom? A quick glance at her face confirmed a similar sentiment.

Two walls and the ceiling had a careful coat of butter-colored paint. The rest was undercoated. One pail held a color called Mexican red. Another beside it contained the butter color.

Eve handed him a baseball cap. "If only you'd come yesterday. My arms nearly dropped off doing the ceiling."

Conn picked up a brush, thumbing the bristles apart. At least she knew the importance of proper brush cleaning. "I'll cut in, if you like." He slapped the cap on his head backward.

Eve began to stir the Mexican red, a deep terracotta. He watched, noting her frequent surreptitious looks at him in the mirror. Their eyes met, and she flushed almost as deeply as the paint.

"You look different in casual clothes," she offered with a shrug.

Conn scrutinized her as she squatted, stirring. "You don't look much like Eve Summers on Channel One, yourself." He leaned back and pointedly checked out the overalls stretched snugly across her shapely rump. "Not that I'm complaining."

Eve straightened, still blushing, and nodded at the pail. She picked up her paint tray and roller and moved across to the other wall. He busied himself positioning the ladder and pouring paint into a tray. For a while they worked in silence. His back was to her and he was several rungs up the ladder but still had a good view in the mirror of her slender body stretching and twisting with every stroke, the big sheet-covered bed between them. Pity it wasn't summer, he mused. There wasn't nearly enough skin on display.

A dollop of paint thudded wetly onto his shirtsleeve, reminding him to take care.

Eve expelled an impatient breath at a strand of hair tickling her cheek. She was hot and bothered, but exertion had little to do with it. Why did she have to be painting this room, today of all days? He could have called a couple of days ago when she was ministering to the bathroom.

But she was pleased to see him. Their last meeting ended awkwardly, but his generous gift and showing up here today suggested he was interested in broadening the relationship. Was it just friendship or had he decided he was ready to do the running?

"How did you get into television?" he asked suddenly.

She didn't turn around. "Right place, right time. I was looking for a producing role, but my face fit and I hit it off with the boss."

Eve and her ex-boss had enjoyed a warm relationship, and she'd repaid his faith in her well by taking the fledgling show to the top of the ratings.

"It wasn't a lifelong ambition?"

She shook her head. "I started off in journalism school. Then while backpacking around Eastern Europe, I stumbled into production. I loved that side of it—still do. Deciding on the leads, a bit of editing, organizing the accommodation and drivers and so on."

"Stumbling into presenting, stumbling into producing—one might think you were a touch clumsy."

Eve flicked him a wry grin through the mirror. A half smile softened the square jaw but he was intent on the wall, giving her the opportunity for a leisurely inspection. "I loved every minute," she murmured, enjoying the different perspective from down here of long, strong legs braced against the top third of the ladder. She had always found him impressive but had not fully appreciated what a spectacular butt he had, especially in worn denims. Man, those shoulders must be an aircraft wing-span across, unconstrained by business jacket or overcoat. His sleeves were rolled up to his elbows, and he was much too tanned for a businessman. Eve toyed with a daydream of messing his plain pale-blue shirt up so he would have to take it off.

She swiped at her hot forehead again. This room was way too small for the likes of him. He was too much, if not physically, then perceptually. Too much blood in his veins or something...

She tore her gaze away. Not considering herself a particularly sensual person, what were the chances of two mind-blowing sexual attractions in one lifetime? What were the chances of one of them working out?

Don't trust lust.

"Is that when you stumbled into marriage?"

Her heart banged hard, obliterating the caution she had just summoned. So he wanted to get personal. Eve knew it was dangerous but blushed with pleasure all the same. "Mmm. In Kosovo. He was—is—an anchor for the BBC. I was the producer."

"What happened?"

How much should she divulge? "We changed." Eve rubbed her nose. "No, I changed. He didn't. He was a ladies' man when we met and he is to this day." She felt his keen interest but kept her eyes on her work.

"Go on."

"I went to England, wanting some roots, a home of some kind. Got a job on breakfast TV, bought a house. But being in the field was in his blood. He couldn't leave it. I should have known that. He came home every few weeks for a visit. It wasn't very long before I started to hear the rumors."

"And you came home."

"Not right away. I confronted him. He begged my forgiveness which I willingly gave, the first time."

"How many times?" he asked quietly.

Eve shrugged. "Two or three."

It wasn't even an ache anymore, more a sense of failure—and her own naiveté. The ache came later, after the first weeks of torrid lovemaking that followed their arguments. She became pregnant—and she hadn't planned it. It was pure accident and carelessness. That is what lust did.

But Conn didn't need to know that right now.

"He did love me in his own way, I think. He followed me here and we tried again. But New Zealand is much smaller, the rumors louder."

Too late, she thought, Conn would know that better than anyone. "It's history. I took a gamble on him changing. It didn't pay off." She heard the stroke of his brush slow, then start up again.

"You like to gamble?" Conn asked.

"I think you have to give people the benefit of the doubt."

"I think three times is more than just being nice. It's nice with a streak of sado-masochism."

She smiled to herself. He was probably right.

"How come your generosity doesn't extend to Pete Scanlon?"

Her head snapped up. "Because he's *still* a louse!" Way to spoil the mood, Buster. "You'll see."

Conn squinted at her from above, his lips pursed thoughtfully. Then that lovely mouth softened. "I'll say one thing. You're a tenacious little thing when you get your teeth into something."

Eve relaxed a little. Pete Scanlon was not going to ruin her day. "Do you like to gamble?"

Conn turned back to his painting. "I bet you already know the answer to that."

A neat stall, if she'd ever heard one. Eve wondered if she should admit knowing a few details of his past, but it was the present she was interested in right now.

"Why would you assume I know anything about you?"

"You're a reporter," he told her with a sniff of disdain. "I'd think it remiss if you weren't delving into people's private lives."

He'd made this personal by bringing up her marriage. Eve went one step further. "We gossip columnists would starve if we had to rely on your exploits of late."

"What is it you want to hear, Eve?" he asked mildly. "Clandestine involvements? Juicy, messy breakups? Or am I still struggling with my demons?" His look was more haughty than heated. "If it's a story you're after, you're out of luck. The stadium takes up all my time."

"Now there's an excuse I've used before," she scoffed. "Throwing yourself into work so you don't have time to think about it. I've been there. It's only now, since I was...since I left my job, that I'm realizing it's time to face up. Deal with things instead of putting them away in a little box for later." She put her roller down. "It's later," she quipped.

He did not reply.

They were finished in an hour and a half, meeting in a corner. Conn was still on his ladder, momentarily trapping her.

"That's called being painted into a corner," she muttered, amused.

"Hang on." He frowned down at her. "I'm just... about..." He finished the piece he was on and then came down, balancing the tray and roller and rag. Eve inhaled appreciatively as his warmth and masculine scent edged through the strong paint smell. His big form descended, one foot at a time, right in front of her. She kept her eyes level, drinking in the tawny skin of his throat, his strong chin, unsmiling mouth, crisp sideburns that made her fingers curl with sultry longing.

Then he turned, bending to lay the tray and roller down. Her fingers gripped the cool metal ladder while she stared at an equally mesmerizing back view. She pursed her lips in an under-the-breath whistle and wrenched her eyes away.

"Whoops," Conn said, right beside her, so close she was afraid he would hear her heart thumping. She felt so flushed. Could be the paint setting her alight, maybe an allergic reaction. When his finger brushed her neck, she couldn't help flinching.

"Easy," he breathed. "Got a spot—right—here." He rubbed gently while she tilted her head back a little, the tension in her neck screaming.

"There."

Released, Eve tottered back a step. "Great. This is great." The words came out in a demented rush. "We're finished." She turned her back, pretending to survey their work.

"What about the windows?"

Eve shook her head. There was only so much close proximity she could take. "Another day."

Conn walked over to the bed, wiping his hands on a rag. "I'll help you move the bed."

Still facing the wall, Eve closed her eyes. Not the damn bed! When she eventually turned, he was facing her, waiting. They lifted and heaved, and when it was in its place, he whipped the paint-spattered sheeting off with a flourish.

Her king-size bed lay between them with its gold and red coverlet and multihued cushions.

Eve stared down, wishing he hadn't done that. Now it was a bed, not a sheet-covered mass in the middle of the room.

Conn was still bent over the bed. She watched as his hands spread wide and glided over the coverlet, smoothing the wrinkles, roughing up her heartbeat. He raised his eyes to hers. There were no underlying messages now. He was brazen in his pupil-darkening awareness, his sardonic amusement of the desire he saw in her face.

Her long-sleeved tee prickled and agitated every millimeter of skin. The very air between them had sex on its breath.

Don't trust lust!

Eve swallowed hard. Her voice, when she spoke, sounded perfectly normal. "You know, I owe you big-time. How about I buy you lunch? In fact, my poor car is going stir-crazy on the mainland. Let's go across so I can take her for a spin."

He couldn't object to her driving, could he?

He looked like he was going to. Then he nodded. "Where can I wash up?"

Five

Eve picked up her car and drove them to the port for lunch. Away from the confines of her bedroom, the tension eased for the most part, returning only when the conversation lapsed. Luckily Eve was a master of conversation.

Conn scowled when their lunch was interrupted by an enthusiastic diner.

"We've missed you on TV, when are you coming back?" the woman gushed.

Alerted by Conn's dark expression, Eve kept the conversation pleasant but brief.

"Does that happen to you a lot?" he asked when they were alone.

"A minute or two out of my day doesn't hurt anyone."

He didn't look convinced.

"Why does it bother you?"

"Because it's bad manners. They should write you a letter," he suggested in a cool tone.

Eve understood his reaction more than he knew, but would not let something so trivial spoil their day. "Just because I have the most beautiful mail box in the country."

Conn could not hide his reluctant grin.

Pleased to see it, she smiled back. "Is Conn feeling left out?"

He shook his head. "I can do without that sort of attention."

"Any sort of attention, perhaps?"

"Perhaps." His eyes were amused but alert.

Eve saw no reason to hide the fact she was interested. "I told you a little of me. Tell me something of you."

"Maybe I'm not the charming, friendly, interesting person you think," he said with a wry twist to his lips.

"Interesting, certainly," she murmured.

He fixed her with a candid gaze. "I'll tell you this. I'd like to know a lot more about you."

Her heart leaped, giving her courage. "We have some common ground, at last." She raised her glass and toasted him. "Make it something— personal."

He leaned back in his seat and crossed his legs. "You sure are pushy, do you know that?"

"You started it." She gave him an encouraging smile, but he was looking across the room. "In your own good time."

"Thanks."

Seconds ticked by but as usual, her curiosity had no patience. He had just admitted he liked her, wanted to know more about her. There was much she wanted to discover too. "You don't drive because of the accident?"

The humor in his face faded fast. "In my own good time, as long as it meets with your deadline?"

She rested her elbows on the table, watching him. So she was naturally curious.

"I drive. I don't particularly like it, and I prefer not to drive anyone else, but when I have to, I do." He frowned. "As you know. Anything else?"

Eve nodded. She was making ground. "Have you had any…" She paused, mentally crossing her fingers and wondering how much of an inflection to put on the next word. "…*serious* relationships since the accident?"

He still wasn't looking at her. His fingernail tapped the side of his glass, making an ominous, brittle sound.

"If you're asking whether everything is in good working order since the accident, I think I'll keep that to myself for now." Then his eyes raked her face. Cool, sea green. Full of warning. "I'd hate to spoil the anticipation."

Any normal person would be two miles away now, running for their lives. His Artic tone rang in her ears, dousing but not wholly diminishing her heated embarrassment. "I wasn't actually…" she stammered. How could he think that was what she meant?

Damn. He was right. She was too pushy.

A couple more taps on his glass and he released her from his gaze and looked down at the table. "One. Short-lived." He pursed his lips. "She said I was a cold, unfeeling bastard."

Eve relaxed a little. She thought she'd blown it there for a moment. "Did that bother you?"

He looked down at his tapping hand. "That she dumped me or that she said that?"

"Both."

His eyes searched her face as if he could find the answer there. Then that brooding mouth softened and he shook his head.

Eve shifted in her chair, more than a little relieved. She smiled at him and something passed between them. A truce. An acceptance of their attraction and past events that could not be changed. She leaned down and picked up her bag. "Let's go see your stadium."

"The contractors don't work on a Sunday. It will be all locked up."

"We can walk around the outside."

Flinty clouds smothered the sun by the time they got to the stadium. They tugged on jackets against the chill wind and walked slowly around the massive enclosure. Conn's pride was evident as he pointed out where the corporate facilities would be, state-of-the-art seating for seventy-five thousand patrons, and the fully retractable roof. It was not large by international standards but New Zealand's small population could not support a bigger structure. Eve was not rabid about rugby but even she recognized this would be a magnificent stadium to rival the world's best. "Why construction?" she asked. It seemed a curious progression from professional sportsman to building. "Most ex-sportsmen go into coaching or writing tell-all books."

Conn shrugged. "I had some money. I wanted to make something. No one makes anything anymore. After the car accident, I bought a struggling three-man construction company and turned it around."

"You got Businessman of the Year three or four years ago," she mused, recalling an article she had read. "Why didn't you accept the award?"

"I did accept it. I didn't go to the awards ceremony, that's all."

"How many people work for you?"

"I have no idea. Hundreds." He pulled his collar up around his neck.

Eve stared in through the enclosure. "Where's your office?"

"In town." He moved his head in the general direction of the city center.

"Where?" Eve stood in front of him, facing the city. She felt his hands on her upper arms, turning her slightly. His arm stretched over her shoulder, finger pointing.

He could have been pointing at the moon for all she noticed. He was so close, each vertebra of her spine could feel his warmth. Too aware to move or even breathe, she fought against leaning back to nestle her head into his throat. He won't be pushed, she reminded herself. *"I'll do the running…"*

So she forced herself to take one step forward and another, keeping her eyes on her feet. They sauntered back toward the car, Eve kicking up little showers of pebbles. When she heard Conn's sharp inhalation, she looked up. A middle-aged couple stood a few feet away from Eve's car.

Conn stopped. "Mum!"

The woman's face broke into a warm smile.

"Hello, love." She took a tentative step forward. Eve saw that the man—Conn's father, she assumed—had turned also but hung back.

"What brings you two here?" Conn walked up, and the woman raised her face to him. He pecked her cheek, then nodded at his father and shoved his hands in his pockets.

"We come often," his mother was saying, doing her best to peer around Conn's bulk at Eve. "Your father likes to check on progress."

"Ah." As if suddenly remembering Eve's presence, Conn turned and drew her in. "This is…"

"Eve Summers!" His mother's smile was delighted. She was a short, shapely woman, nothing like her son in physicality, but the smile was pure Conn Bannerman, only a lot more ready.

Eve held out her hand, shrugging off Conn's murmured "Drumm, actually."

"Goodness it's nice to meet you," his mother beamed. "We're such fans of yours at home. The girls at my golf club will be green with envy."

"Nice of you to say, Mrs. Bannerman." Eve shook the woman's hand and turned to Conn's father. "Mr. Bannerman."

He, too, had little of Conn's size or coloring, being much darker. Taller than Eve but nowhere near as broad as his rugby-playing son, though she knew he too had been a rugby star in his youth. He had the same structure of face and the same remarkable green eyes.

Except that while Conn's simmered with desire, snapped with anger or clouded over with distance, the older man's eyes seemed—disheartened.

"Dad thought you might have finished the west stand by now."

Mr. Bannerman grunted and turned to face the enclosure. Deftly the woman moved behind her son to stand beside Eve. Conn stepped up beside his father, hands still in his pockets.

"What do you think of it?" Mrs. Bannerman asked. "Is this your first visit?"

"It's going to be fantastic," Eve enthused.

Mrs. Bannerman sighed with relief when the two men

began walking alongside the enclosure. Conn dragged his hand from his pocket occasionally to point something out, as he had done with Eve. Progress was slower. Mr. Bannerman obviously had more educated questions to ask, although Conn displayed none of the pride and enthusiasm he had shown on her guided tour.

Eve and his mother followed. She learned they drove up from their dairy farm about ninety minutes south most weekends to check on progress at the new Gulf Harbor Stadium.

"How did you two meet?"

"I'm his new neighbor."

"Not the old Baxter place? Did you buy it? I thought my son had plans for that place."

"Mmm. I think I'm the spanner in the works," Eve told her wryly.

His mother laughed. "Connor may have built himself a grand fortress now but he grew up in a farmhouse. It was a bit bigger than yours but about the same era."

"And hopefully in much better shape than mine. Conn's been helping me paint today."

Mrs. Bannerman rocked back on her heels, looking incredulous. "Really?" Then her face split into another beaming smile.

It was Eve's turn to be taken aback when the older woman slipped an arm in hers and began walking slowly again. "I'm so glad he has a friend. Connor made me give up matchmaking for him years ago."

"Don't measure me up for the family plot yet," Eve laughed. "Your son has no time for media people."

"No. He doesn't." Mrs. Bannerman squeezed her arm. "It's been difficult for him." She lowered her tone with a quick glance at the men ahead. "You know about the accident?"

Eve nodded. "I feel bad that the media seemed so unforgiving at the time."

They walked slower, lagging behind. Eve learned that Conn was subjected to immense scrutiny because his father was a former national player. He was also the youngest player ever selected for the national team.

"He was not yet nineteen when he made the team. It was a huge change for him, coming as he did from a modest country home to all the attention, money—and the women! Enough to turn anyone's head."

The public grew tired of back-to-back losing seasons and began to bay for the players' blood. They were labeled spoiled prima donnas. Conn by then was dating the darling of New Zealand's only soap opera, Rachel Lee. That made him even more of a target for the paparazzi.

The accident that killed her, and for which he was responsible, was the last nail in his coffin as far as the media was concerned.

Eve recalled the news clippings her friend had sent. Many of them were hateful. It was an accident for which he had paid dearly, but to the newspapers covering the tragedy, he should have been strung up.

The men stopped and turned. They looked as if they would rather be anywhere else, but Mrs. Bannerman had other ideas. "Why don't we go find an early dinner somewhere, the four of us?"

Eve started to agree.

"We've just eaten," Conn said quickly.

The desolation in his father's face floored her, but he said nothing.

"A drink, then," Mrs. Bannerman said, and Eve thought she'd never heard such pleading.

"I could murder for a coffee," she said, giving her arms a brisk rub. "I'm freezing."

In the face of defeat, Conn distantly acquiesced. Eve followed the Bannermans' car to a nearby hotel, and they ordered coffee and cake and Conn and his father a beer.

Mrs. Bannerman pointed out a pool table in the bar area. "You two used to love thrashing each other at pool. Go have a game."

Eve wanted to ask why the relationship was so strained, but she felt guilty that she'd forced Conn's hand to agree to come for a coffee. In any event, she did not have to ask. Mrs. Bannerman volunteered the details.

"We used to be such a happy family. Connor and his sister, Erin, were the best of friends, and he worshipped his father. They were inseparable." She looked over at the quiet pair playing pool. "Look at them now. They can't even look at each other."

"But why? Surely his father doesn't blame Conn...?"

His mother shook her head. "Nobody in the family blames Connor. They don't have to. He blames himself. His guilt just eats away. And although his dad misses him more than he would miss me if I died, Connor feels he's disappointed him, let him down. We have tried for ten years to reach him, show him how proud we are of him. Because—" she looked at Eve earnestly "—he is a *good man,* Eve. A really good man, despite his refusal to enjoy life." She sighed as if her heart would break. "But he won't have it. He shuts himself in his fortress and pushes everyone away. There is nothing we can do, and no success or achievement of his makes him feel any different."

* * *

On the way home Eve noted that Conn responded minimally to her chatter. When she asked him in, he declined politely, saying he had paperwork to catch up on, though he did thank her for lunch and said he'd had a good time.

In a way, she was relieved. She wanted some quiet time to think about the revelations of the day. When she got inside, her machine was beeping. There was a message from Grant, her old boss, saying he would try later. He sounded agitated. Worried, Eve tried to call him, but the line was engaged.

She lit the fire. The house was cold because she had left all the windows open to dissipate the strong paint smell. The bedroom looked great. Only the door molding and window sills to do now and she should get through that tomorrow. She wondered if Conn would offer to help.

Conn Bannerman. Successful, wealthy, spectacularly handsome. Would he close himself up in his little world—fortress—forever? An overpowering attraction was one thing, but Eve's feelings seemed to be growing into a complication she could do without right now. It was not her mission to lead him out of the maze of guilt he had lost himself in. If his family couldn't do it, what chance did she have?

Eve paced the room moodily, trying to focus on the next step of her renovations. She needed a project, something to occupy her mind, but projects were short-term things. Intuition warned her that there was nothing short-term about the feelings flourishing inside for her aloof neighbor.

Conn whistled along to music while struggling with his bow tie. He didn't wear the damn things often enough to become proficient at tying them.

But he wouldn't let the recalcitrant tie get him down tonight. It was too long since he had seen her, three days. Over those three days, Conn had accepted that Eve was not going anywhere, either from old Baxter's place or from a compartment in his mind he'd thought was sealed.

She had called him the day before with an intriguing invitation. Her newspaper had been furnished with tickets to a mayoral-campaign fund-raiser evening. She laughed gaily, telling him whose fund-raiser it was. "Come with me. I'd behave myself if you were there, glowering at me."

"Liar," he'd scoffed. "You want protection in case Scanlon—quite rightly—throws you out on your ear."

"I cannot believe he was naive enough to think the *New City* wouldn't give me the tickets. They're getting a lot of mileage out of my columns."

Conn grudgingly acquiesced, but he made her work for it, telling her he had already turned down Pete's official invite. Eve did not seem to care that there might be a conflict of interest in her and Conn, from opposing sides of the fence, going together.

He pulled his coat on over his tux, turned off the new CD he had purchased yesterday and set off on the short walk down the hill. What would she be wearing—businesslike or sexy? Would they dance, or just dance around the fact that they wanted each other?

Nothing he conjured up in his mind prepared him for the pleasure of her appearance. It was a suit—the color of an aged pewter mug. The straight skirt was almost to her ankles and she wore ludicrously high pumps. The jacket was the eye-catcher. Very low cut, a kind of double-hemmed thing with scalloped edges and tightly buttoned. And there was no blouse under it to take away the effect of luscious cleavage. Only a thin band of silver with a cluster of black pearls lay against her skin.

She looked flustered, ushering him in and rushing from one side of the room to another. "Sorry I'm late," she apologized, tossing her hair back and fixing matching black pearl earrings. "I had a phone call and it took ages…you look great, by the way. Should we book a cab from the terminal now?"

Conn shook his head. "My driver is meeting us."

Eve seemed distracted by something on the ferry trip but shook her head when he inquired if anything was wrong, and he put it down to nerves at coming face-to-face with her childhood enemy. While she chewed on her sexy bottom lip and stared at the approaching lights of the city, Conn leaned toward her, inhaling deeply of an exquisite fragrance. Smoky tropical flowers? Whatever, it was quite different to the lemony fragrance he had come to associate with Eve.

"What's he going to do when he sees you tonight?" he asked in a low voice. Perversely low so that she leaned closer to hear him.

"I have no idea," Eve confessed. She continued to worry her lip and he was hard-pressed not to chide her, as if he had some proprietary right over her mouth.

When they got to the function, he helped her out of the car and told the driver he would call for the return trip. Cameras flashed around the entrance to the theater, site of the fund-raising dinner. Conn grimaced but Eve took his arm and they sailed through with only scant interest.

Once inside, Eve was almost immediately drawn into conversation with some TV contacts. Conn took a predinner drink and watched admiringly as she worked her charm. In no time at all it seemed there was a line of people waiting to catch her eye and exchange a word.

How different they were, he thought. He spoke for a couple of minutes to an advertising agency executive of his acquaintance, traded nods with several councillors and was content to stand back and admire Eve's social skills.

As he raised his glass, he saw Pete Scanlon approach. His eyes flicked over to Eve. She was nearby but not looking their way.

This should be interesting....

"Conn! Great you could make it." The older man pumped his hand.

"Last-minute thing."

There was something wrong. Conn did not know Pete Scanlon well, but he'd always impressed him as a cool customer, elegant, charming, poised. Tonight the man was clearly agitated. A sheen of sweat gleamed on his wide forehead, and his hand was damp. His eyes were never still, flicking here and there as if expecting a catastrophe to descend.

"By the way," Conn added, "I'd prefer no public announcement of my contributions if you don't mind."

Pete waved his hand. "No problem."

Eve had looked over and was now attempting to extricate her hand from a woman's grip. Conn held his breath as she approached. Pete was in the middle of a rambling expression of gratitude for Bannerman, Inc.'s support when Eve took her place beside Conn and faced her enemy with her head held high.

Pete's eyes flicked to her face and away—and then snapped back. His mouth all but dropped open. "Well, well. If it isn't little Miss Ear Drumm."

Conn's head jerked up. "What did you say?" His voice sounded hoarse to his own ears.

"It's okay, Conn." Eve put a hand on his arm. "It was my nickname when I was growing up. I don't mind."

Conn stared at the man, suddenly seeing him as he never had before.

Pete's eyes moved from one to the other, comprehension dawning. "Sleeping with my enemy, Conn? A figure of speech, of course," he added quickly, possibly seeing the tense warning in Conn's face. "I'm surprised—yes, and a little disappointed. But I do hope you will continue to be a generous supporter once the election is won. When I'm a friend, I'm a friend for life."

Conn stared at him coldly, still trying to swallow the man's first words to Eve.

"Gee, Pete, you're looking a bit peaked," Eve said lightly. "Is it the strain of public office? Or perhaps a few poison arrows are coming home to roost?"

Pete smiled but his eyes glinted with dislike. Conn saw for the first time what she must see when she looked at him: a heavy-set bully who manipulated and greased his way through life.

"Your escort is welcome to stay, Miss Drumm. You, however, lost any right to be here when you started your malicious little column. I'll thank you to leave."

"My pleasure, Pete. I think you've just about outstayed your welcome in this city, anyway. This party stinks." Eve's voice rang out, causing a couple nearby to look over. But there was enough of a hubbub in the room to cover their raised voices.

Conn watched as she moved a step closer, raised her hand and tapped his glass. "Still on the whiskey, I see. I hope little Josh's babysitter has her own wheels tonight."

An ugly sneer twisted Pete's mouth. "Little Josh is a bit

big for babysitters these days. But you were the best baby-sitter *I* ever had."

The blood drained from Conn's head quicker than a snap of the fingers. "That's *it!*" he grated and moved toward the odious man.

Eve was quicker. Just as he reached out to grab at Pete's tie, she stepped right in the middle of the two men, facing Conn, her slight frame jammed in between their bodies. "Don't give him the satisfaction." Her eyes pleaded with him, her hands pressed on his chest, her body tight and tense as his.

With her intervention Pete was able to step back, tugging his tie out of reach.

"*Please,* Conn."

He flicked his eyes at her face through a haze of red that slowly cleared. His exhalation was careful, aware that he was one second away from losing control.

He looked back to Scanlon's face. The man shuffled, his face flushed to a dull brick. Conn slid his wallet from his jacket pocket and flourished a coin. He flicked it expertly and it spun high. Pete, Eve and the curious couple nearby all leaned their heads back, their eyes following the spinning silver up and up before it gave in to gravity. Twinkling, it came down with a sharp musical clink and splosh! right into Pete's heavy crystal glass.

He flinched. Amber liquid shot out of his glass, splashing his front. The party chatter seemed to be absorbed by the air.

"My donation for the drink," Conn said clearly. "And that's the last cent you'll see from me."

Someone tittered behind them as they marched out of the function room and into the lobby. Eve laughed, high and shaky. "Some exit," she whispered, leaning close. "We have to queue for the coat check."

But Conn's glower at the assistant had her running to get their coats in the middle of serving another patron. He flipped his cell phone open to call his driver.

Eve took his arm. "Let's walk. It's only ten minutes."

He grunted and called the driver to cancel. A long-haired photographer moved toward them, camera rising.

Eve had a tight grip on his arm. "Just walk," she muttered. Turning her most brilliant smile on the man, she bade him a cheery good-night and steered them both down the street.

They didn't speak again until they hit the waterfront and discovered there was plenty of time for the next ferry.

"Drink?"

She shrugged. They walked slowly past every bar and restaurant on the Viaduct Basin down to the deserted dark end of the wharf where the ferries docked. Conn didn't know about her, but he'd had enough of people for one night.

Eve released his arm and they stood side by side looking out to sea. He could see the stiffness in her shoulders, her white-knuckled grip on the railing. If hers was anything like the tension draining out of him, it felt like tomorrow they'd both be nursing aching shoulder, neck and jaw muscles.

He leaned forward with his hands clasped and hanging over the railing.

"My hero," she said, her voice almost inaudible. He turned his head to find her looking at him. Inexplicably, her eyes brimmed and she looked down, putting her forehead on her hands for a moment.

Conn wanted to grab her and hold her. Or glower and demand she pull herself together.

"Thirteen years since I've seen him, and I know it's wrong to hate someone, but I hate him."

"Not wrong," Conn said lamely.

A light breeze shifted her hair but didn't cover the perplexed expression. "Did you see him? He's really rattled."

Conn nodded. "Even before he saw you, he was sweating. Looks like he's got a lot on his mind."

"Maybe things are unraveling. I had a strange call tonight before we came out. My ex-boss, Grant, has gone missing. His wife is frantic. He left me a really weird emotional message three days ago. Said he'd call back, but he hasn't. She told me he's been in a state for weeks."

"What's that to do with Scanlon?"

"I've discovered that Pete has his hooks into a lot of important people, including TV people. I know Grant hated sacking me but he would not agree to have me explore Pete's corruption on air, and I wouldn't back off."

That was a surprise. "You were sacked? I thought you quit."

"That was the official line. Grant gave me that option in case I ever wanted to work in TV again."

She faced him, her arm lying along the railing close to him. "I also found out that one of the station's directors is close to Pete. I'm guessing it's all connected somehow."

Conn straightened and looked down at her hands, wondering if they were cold. "I'm glad I found out what a jerk he is before I sank any more money into him."

She made a small sound of agreement, but her eyes were on his big hand inching toward hers on the rail.

Man, but she was lovely to look at. Not just the usual feminine attributes, of which she was abundantly endowed. It was her wholesome vitality. The life in her—warmth and strength and vulnerability. She'd had her knocks but they hadn't kept her down. She was generous and optimistic, and she somehow filled a space in him. When had he last been so entranced by a woman?

His fingers slid the last millimeter until they touched hers. The resulting jolt of energy was powerful but not enough so he didn't notice her fingers still and tense. He knew he shouldn't but he did it anyway, lifted his hand and placed it over hers.

He had *never* been so entranced by a woman and that was the sad truth. With his self-imposed exile from a social life, he cut his chances of being entranced by about ninety-nine percent.

Eve seemed to move closer into his side. Again that powerful force to kiss her rocked him. What was stopping him? There was no one around.

He'd started out this evening looking forward to being with her. Maybe moving things to their logical conclusion; that being, taking her to his bed. Then he could concentrate on the very big job at hand instead of spending his days and nights obsessing about her.

He did not usually sleep with women he would be likely to bump into again. But then, he didn't expect Eve to be a permanent fixture on the island. She was a people person and a television celebrity. Soon she would be bored with that ramshackle, damp old house and hanker for the city lights.

And that would be that.

"Conn?"

Blinking, he looked into her questioning eyes. That would be that. She couldn't live in his world, and he sure as hell couldn't be part of hers.

"You're miles away," she was saying.

"I'm right here."

She moved her hand. It slid against his, causing a friction that tightened his skin. All of it. The blood started flowing faster when she didn't take her hand away.

"I know the stadium is important to you," Eve said.

Nothing's as important to me right now as kissing you, having you, he thought savagely.

"Can't you sweet-talk the mayor?" she continued. "Have you tried? Benson may be old and stale but there's no question of his loyalty to the people of this city."

He frowned down at their hands, then laced their fingers lightly, sliding his up slowly until he reached the web of hers.

Even when she spread her fingers, it was a tight fit. A licentious thrill went through him at that thought, and he inhaled very carefully, grateful it didn't come out as a groan. "Not much of a sweet-talker, actually, Eve."

He turned her hand over and stroked her palm, heard the little jagged hitch in her breath that signaled her excitement. When he looked at her, her soft, full lips were moist and inviting.

Conn swallowed and unclenched his jaw. "This is getting out of hand," he murmured, and pulled her toward him. Forget preliminaries. Her mouth opened for him, her free hand was already reaching for his hair. He swirled his tongue around hers and sucked, releasing her hand and wrapping her up as close as she could be.

"Hey, Ms. Summers," an indolent voice said, just before Conn forgot himself completely and lifted her to grind his aching body against her.

Eve inhaled sharply and pulled back. Then the world exploded. They sprang apart, blinded by the powerful flash.

Conn's eyes took a second to adjust, and he squinted at

the origin of the voice, recognizing the same photographer who had approached them at the fund-raiser. Young, unkempt, wearing a big heavy camera in front of him and an ugly sneer.

As disbelief, frustration and anger surged, he gripped Eve's shoulders and put her body away from him.

"Conn," she warned, and she knew him well enough to sound worried.

He didn't care. He was going to enjoy this. "You like to swim, punk?"

Eve dragged on his arm when he took a step toward the guy. He lifted his arm, annoyed, and the youth turned and ran. Conn gathered himself to bound after him but did not reckon on the persistence of Eve, feet planted on the ground with a two-handed desperate hold on his sleeve.

"Don't be silly. You'll make things worse."

Conn's head rolled back, and he swore savagely.

"It would have been a lousy shot," she told him. "Doubt they'll even use it."

Conn swore again, rubbing his face. "Do you know him? What rag is he from?"

She shook her head.

He was blowing like he'd just done sixty minutes on the rowing machine. Was it sexual excitement or rage that had him so pumped?

"Conn?"

Eve's discomfort showed in the way she used her teeth to drag her bottom lip into her mouth, over and over. "It's not so bad, is it? I mean, we're both single…"

"That's not the point." He frowned down at his watch. "Better get to the terminal." He strode off, still flushed with disused adrenaline, leaving her standing there.

Eve caught up with him. "Okay, before that, I was going to suggest something. Maybe some publicity for the stadium."

Conn sighed. "My people are on it," he told her shortly, really not in the mood to talk.

Eve reached out and grabbed one of his hands. "Yes, but, if we made it more about people, less about business…"

Conn came to a halt. Her touch warmed him and warned him. This was crazy, too much of a complication. She was his neighbor. She was a celebrity and a gossip columnist. He wanted—he would—push her away because she had the capacity to infiltrate and wreak havoc on his ordered routine.

He turned to her. "There's no story here, Eve," he said roughly, tugging his hand from hers. "There's the ferry."

She stared at him, hurt showing in her eyes. Conn hated that, but it was about time she learned what sort of man he was. She had no business getting mushy over him.

They spoke little on the way home. She was subdued, he hard-hearted and resentful.

And totally frustrated. The skin of her cleavage glowed, as if she'd captured the moon inside. His hands itched to take each side of the delicate curved jacket and rip it apart to bare her. She'd crossed one leg over the other, and even her elegantly clad foot aroused him as it nodded to some beat in her head.

Her scent had softened into an addictive subtlety that had him lean his head back and close his eyes, purely for the torture of filling another of his senses. Life was cruel indeed to throw every man's dream woman practically into his lap and then make him say no.

Especially when *she* wouldn't say no, and they both knew it.

They did not speak in the cab, either. Conn wondered

if he would be strong enough to let her out. Or not to jump out after her when they got to her house.

Eve fussed in her bag for money.

"I've got it," he grated, irritated because he knew that both of them had a picture in mind for this moment, and this wasn't it.

Disgusted with himself because it had to be this way.

She looked at him, and in the moonlight her eyes were confused and disappointed. "Thanks." She didn't move.

He didn't speak. Moments ticked by. The cab driver sighed.

"Just one thing, Conn," Eve said very softly. "Were you in love with the actress?"

He exhaled and searched her face. That was the last thing he'd expected. Then he shook his head. "I couldn't handle the publicity."

She nodded, still looking at him, but her hand reached behind her, fumbling for the door handle.

"I still can't," he added with finality, and watched the confusion flow into regret. She blinked and was gone.

The bourbon was smooth, the night cool on his deck above the ocean, but Conn burned with a restless tension that he couldn't shake. You could have had her tonight! With one word from him, he would not be standing here alone fantasizing about her in his arms, him in her body.

So do it! Get it over with. Finish it once and for all. Because it *would* finish it for him, once he'd slept with her. There was no other way ahead, no future for them. Get her out of your system and out of your head.

He took a swallow, chased it down with another lungful of the expensive cigars he smoked every couple of months.

"Hello, Eve," he said to the universe, imagining her face when he knocked on her door. "If you don't make love to me tonight, it will kill me."

The smoke curled satisfyingly around his lungs as he visualized her gentle acquiescence, saw the answering desire in her eyes.

Six

The message light on her answering machine blinked as she swung through the lounge and into the kitchen. A tension headache sent little brow-wrinkling spots of pain behind her eyes. She filled a glass of water, flipped her recording switch on and flopped down on the sofa.

"Ms. Drumm, I'm calling from the *Herald*. Can you call me as soon as you get in? Doesn't matter what time." The voice gave a name and number and then there was silence.

What could she want? It was early but Eve didn't feel like talking to anyone, except maybe the man up the hill. Her disappointment at the way the evening ended— alone—was too keen to focus on anything else.

She rummaged in her evening bag for aspirin, pausing as the machine beeped again. "Hey, hon, it's Lesley. Call me, okay? Anytime."

Eve sighed, easing her shoes off. Perhaps a girl talk was

just what she needed. She wasn't doing much of a job herself in sorting out her feelings for that man. She wanted him, but she couldn't afford the scars he would inflict on her heart. She wanted to heal his wounded soul, but she had her own stuff to sort out... Conn, Conn, his name went around and around in her head.

Beep! Another reporter, wanting an interview and to talk about a position at a rival TV station. "Interesting times," his voice said enigmatically.

Eve sat up. What interesting times?

Beep! "Eve? It's Grant. Damn! I really needed to talk to you before— Call me, urgently. My cell is..."

Eve repeated the numbers aloud while scribbling them down. At least Grant had turned up.

Beep! A half-dozen more reporters... Eve stood in the middle of her living room, feeling the first stirrings of dread. What was going on?

One last message from Grant. "I'm sorry you had to hear this on the news. At least it's over now."

Alarm hollowed out her stomach. She grabbed the TV remote, checking her watch. Ten-thirty. News time.

There he was, the lead story. Her boss's face was gray with fatigue and emotion. Eve was so shocked at his devastated expression, the words didn't sink in at first, but the mention of Pete Scanlon cleared her head soon enough.

Grant had had a weekend fling with a high-class call girl on one of Pete's chartered yacht trips. The slime had threatened to expose him—unless he sacked Eve.

She had played right into their hands.

Eve backed up till her legs touched the sofa and then eased down, never taking her eyes off the screen. Her own face flashed in front of her, clips from her show. "Our efforts to entice the new mayoral candidate onto the show…" "This unknown burst onto the scene a very short time ago but is already making an impact…"

It became more surreal as Grant made a heartbroken apology to his wife and family, to Eve, to the TV station he had compromised and the viewers he had misled.

The broadcast panned to the theater she and Conn had gone to earlier. There was Pete, hamming it up, greeting people with a wide smile and crushing handshake—but that must have been early. There was no telltale whiskey stain on his shirt.

Eve turned down the sound a little, the elation just beginning to warm her veins.

He was finished, surely. With this stink clinging to him, he must resign. Popular as he was, these revelations would torpedo his dirty rotten campaign, and even Pete could not recover and slime his way out of this. Not in the ten days left till the election.

Good riddance! The city could consider itself extremely lucky.

Eve stood up with one word going through her mind. Dad. "I hope you're watching, Dad," she said aloud, her voice a little choked up.

The announcer's voice cut through her bittersweet fog and she turned the sound back up. Her formerly anonymous contact had come forward, stating there were at least half a dozen prominent citizens prepared to lodge statements with the police about Scanlon's tax consultancy, among other things. He praised Eve's courage and conviction in encouraging these people to come forward.

"Woo-hoo!" She punched the air and did a little twirl.

It felt great to be vindicated, but she owed a debt of gratitude to these brave men.

The news reader wound up: "Mr. Scanlon has refused to make any comment, except to say that he is innocent of all charges. In other news tonight…"

Interesting times indeed.

The phone rang and she snatched it up eagerly. It was a reporter. He was on the ferry and would be at her door in one hour. Was that okay, and if not, he would spend the night in his car and see her in the morning.

Dazed, Eve told him she would see him in the morning. Oh, God. Conn.

What were the implications for him? He had hung his hopes on Pete, though he may have changed his mind tonight. But she could not expect him to see this development as good news. Would he blame her? The broadcast made it sound as if Eve was prominent in the man's downfall, not that she believed that for a minute. Pete Scanlon had made more powerful enemies than her. Still, Conn could conceivably hold her partly responsible for causing him major professional problems.

She picked up the phone, then thought better of calling him. There could be a reporter sitting at her gate shortly. She was about to get a taste of what they call "heat" over the next day or so. Assuming he hadn't heard, she wanted to be with him when he learned of it, hear what he thought of it.

She really wanted to know what he thought of her.

She laced up trainers, grabbed her long woollen overcoat and turned off the lights. A couple of minutes up the hill, she heard the sound of a car. Odd, there was only her and Conn on this ridge. Hugging the shoulder of the gravel road, she heard the car slow and then stop.

Eve turned back for a look. A car was parked at her gate, but no one got out. They turned their lights out. A reporter, no doubt.

She turned and quickened her pace, feeling slightly creeped out.

Thankfully Conn hadn't bothered to close his big iron security gates. She rang the doorbell, undoing the first few buttons of the overcoat. The quick walk up the hill had overheated her. That or her elation—or was it anticipation?

Conn opened the door jacketless, tieless, his shirtsleeves rolled up to his elbows. He held a heavy crystal glass in one hand and a big fat smoking cigar in the other.

It surprised her every time she saw him how much her eyes loved him. She stared rudely, trying to get her breathing under control. A bluish shadow shaded his square jaw. She wanted to feel the rasp of it under her fingers. A frown creased his wide brow. This master of his own fortress looked magnificently displeased at the encroachment of his walls. But as she watched, a decision was being made in his eyes.

Her heartbeat, already labored after her exertions, thumped strongly in her ears. Eve knew only that she wanted to be that decision.

"Celebrating?" she asked softly.

His eyes had been traveling down over her body, pausing at the ludicrous trainers on her feet. They swept back to her face and fried her with a look that was hungry, hunted and predatory at the same time.

Ohmigod! She saw clearly what he was thinking. That she was here because…

He raised his hand and she flinched as his cigar flew over her shoulder onto the footpath. The glass was set down with a bang on the telephone table by the door.

"I am now," he murmured, stepping forward to hook his index finger in the top button of her low-cut jacket.

Eve gulped as his finger burned on her night-cooled skin. Her chest rose and her brain was wiped clear of anything but the anticipation—and apprehension—vibrating through her. Before she could recover, his head came down and he covered her mouth with his.

Bourbon and cigar smoke and pure, unadulterated lust spun through her senses. His hands on either side of her face were warm, his lips cool and sure. His tongue touched her lips, demanding her response, not her permission.

No one had done this to her before, had her spinning so fast, so easily. Conn Bannerman cooked her from the inside. When he kissed, when he touched, she was consumed by vibrant color and music. She couldn't get close enough, kiss deep enough, without losing all sense of time and reason.

She pressed up against him in invitation. Her tongue lashed his. His hands left her face and roamed down her back, pulling her close. She melted against him, so glad to be here. Her heart had already decided; her body fiercely urged her to revel in that decision.

Then he broke the kiss and pulled her inside, and suddenly she had nowhere to go. Her back was against the door, her front against the hard wall of his body.

An annoying jab of conscience pierced her. She would completely forget why she was here if she didn't tell him now. "Conn?" she gasped as he crowded her on the door.

He took her mouth in another deep, deep kiss that set her head reeling, with a sound in the back of his throat that may have been a groan or a grunted response to her question.

Or not…still with his mouth locked on hers, he turned

her ninety degrees, lifted her slightly and then down so that her trainers were atop his shoes. He began to walk. Their knees bumped, and she felt every muscle in those hard thighs propelling them along. His kisses became more urgent, his hands were all over her.

Then he stopped and she registered they were entering a room. His bedroom. He set her down and then whirled her across the room, her feet barely touching the ground. The backs of her legs bumped into something. His bed.

Conn slid his hands inside her overcoat. She ached for skin against skin, burned for it. The overcoat hit the ground.

As she battled for air—life-giving air, not the high-altitude effervescence he allowed her—she wondered how many times she had lived this scenario in her mind? Being taken by him, his taste, his power, the bulk of him pressed against her, urgent and hot. Could she turn her back on this chance to make her dreams come true?

He sucked against the base of her ear, then the pulse point in her throat that pumped against his lips. His fingers began expertly popping her suit jacket buttons from the bottom up, and seconds later the suit jacket was on its way down her arms to join the overcoat crumpled on the floor.

How fast she had fallen, how utterly turned on she was. Her body shrieked to be touched.

But although he was never still, Conn was in no hurry. He leaned back a little, running his hands down her arms. Desire blazed from his eyes as he devoured the sight of her, naked from the waist up except for her bra. Eve had barely touched him at all, time had raced away so quickly. She reached for his shirt fastenings as he reached for her bra. But it seemed every time he took his mouth away from hers, her conscience needled her.

"Conn, I need…" Coherence evaporated when her fumbling finally exposed richly tanned skin, bunched masses of muscle on his chest. Lord, the size of him…for just a second, apprehension clambered all over anticipation. These muscles merely had to twitch and they'd break her in two.

Then her bra strap pinged and loosened abruptly. The release and an aching need to be touched by him spirited her trepidation away. She wanted him. She always had. She faced it, his immense physicality and power was an aphrodisiac.

Conn moved and nipped the side of her throat. "Be right back."

What? Her senses protested bitterly as he walked through a door and disappeared. She sucked in a breath that stuck in her throat and wouldn't be expelled. Just as well or she might have cursed out loud.

She glanced around the huge room. The lights across the harbor were magical, as if the city floated on the water. Her reflection stared despondently back in the ample expanse of uncovered windows. Eve frowned at her bra straps that were still halfway down her arms but then the events of the evening ebbed and flowed in her agitated brain, distracting her. He did not seem surprised to see her, as if he was expecting her. Did he know? Could she turn her back on her conscience and make love with him, knowing that his life project was in jeopardy?

His sudden reflection in the window made her jump and spin to face him. His hair was tousled, his shirt open. He stared back. Open shirt, closed, intense face. His arm came up and a handful of condoms hit the bed, then he was in front of her, cupping her face with both hands.

"I have to tell you something," she whispered, bringing her own hands up to rest on his.

His breath brushed her face. "All the reasons why we shouldn't do this will still be there tomorrow," he said softly. "If you don't want this, Eve, now—with me—keep talking."

Her choice. She inhaled the subtleties of salty skin, heated ardor, danger. The inherently male scents and sensibilities that made a woman want to rub her face over her man. The choice by then was easy. She had tried. Not hard enough, but now she was going to save her life and make love with her cold, aloof neighbor.

Lifting up onto her toes, she pulled his head down and kissed him, with the words "I choose you" hammering through her mind. When he pulled back long moments later, his eyes glowed like a caress that warmed her through, the truest smile he had ever gifted her with.

Then the same insane motion that had so drugged her before rendered her helpless again. His answering kiss was possessive, as if he were entitled—and who was she to argue? She did as he commanded.

Never had she been so pliant. Passive was not her style but she was helpless in the onslaught of his whispered commands, clever hands and burning mouth. She stood trembling, eyes closed, her insides molten with sensation. The words he spoke may have been in her head. *Move your arms. Lift up. Turn around for me.* As he peeled her clothing away, his mouth chased every stitch, his hands molded and caressed. She allowed herself to be swept away, and each kiss, each stroke built her need until she felt she was spiraling out of her mind.

It might have been one minute or ten before he was sliding her panties down, kneading the exquisitely sensitive backs of her thighs, coaxing her legs apart. She tensed against it but the moment he put his mouth *there,* where she yearned for him to be, it seemed she'd been on the edge forever, every cell screaming for release. Her legs locked and she couldn't help it, she shattered within seconds and it almost hurt in its intensity. She clutched his head while he absorbed and contained her tremors with his mouth. Then she floated in indescribable ecstasy, supported by his mouth and hands and not afraid anymore.

She could have stayed like that forever. It was always a little sad when the throb of release ebbed away. But her knees began to tremble, she became aware that her breath was backed up in her lungs and her fingers still gripped his hair.

He rose slowly and even now, neglected barely an inch of her, lazily kissing her stomach and stroking. He'd taken care of his own undressing, though she couldn't have explained how or when. He took her in his arms and swallowed the last of her jagged moans.

"Oh, wow!" Eve whispered shakily. "Too much!"

"Not nearly enough."

She shivered with delicious aftershocks as he reached for protection and then sat on the edge of the bed, pulling her to stand in between his legs. Eve had a glimpse of him, huge, imposing. But before she could do more than wonder "Oh, mama, will I survive?" his hands were on her waist, lifting her up over him. She just had time to clutch at his massive shoulders while he slid a hand under her and slowly lowered her onto himself.

Eve took several shallow breaths that all added up to a mean lungful, and relaxed her grip, allowing him to ease her down. Inch by inch, she took him into her still-quivering body.

Where she would have hurried, hungry for his possession, he firmed his hands on her hips to slow her.

"Too much?" he breathed.

"More," she sighed, burning to feel him inside her.

But he controlled her descent with awesome power in his arms, his eyes reassuring, his kiss heartbreakingly gentle. Her still-exquisitely sensitive flesh would probably thank him tomorrow, she conceded silently—but her excitement had built again so quickly. If she hadn't come a few minutes ago, she would be screaming by now.

Slow, achingly slow, he slid deeper, as deep as she had ever experienced. Her heart pounded, for she know he was still nowhere near as deep as he could go. An impatient breath huffed out of her mouth, and she scissored her legs around his waist. It was his turn to catch his breath. She felt him shift, his thighs bunch under her and the grip on her hips relax slightly. Eve stole the march and gathered herself to thrust down and slickly swallow his whole great length.

They both stopped breathing, watching each other. She tightened tentatively around him, learning his shape, his size, his incredible heat. A single bead of sweat formed on his temple, and in response, her insides liquefied.

He cleared his throat, sounding strangled. "Too much?"

Her hands dropped to his thighs and she leaned back a few inches, exhaling carefully. "Perfect."

It didn't surprise her that he was big. What mattered was that he exercised such care, such powerful control, easing her vulnerabilities. Even hardly moving, he touched places inside her that had never been touched. She moved on him carefully and his thickness chafed that tiny bundle of nerves that took on a heartbeat all of its own. Tensing, she peeled his hands off her hips and brought them to her breasts. "I want to move."

His open palms rubbed over her nipples, and she gasped

and locked her ankles around his waist. But when he leaned forward and took half of her breast into his mouth and sucked, she cried out, slammed by the piercing sensations that rushed through her to fuse with the pulsing where they were joined. All of her past experiences shrank to nothing when he began to thrust, slow but oh so deep. His eyes burned into hers and told her that he, too, was absorbed by the intensity of their connection.

Too intense. She clutched at his neck, holding on physically but giving herself permission to let go mentally. Don't think about next time, next week. Don't think about how incredible this feels, how no one else—ever—will feel like this. It's the jackpot, for sure, and jackpots are once-in-a-lifetime things.

Her first orgasm had shocked her with its sharp unexpectedness. Now something hummed and swelled, closing in on her, slowly overtaking her in a toe-curling sweep of sensation that rippled from the tips of her toes to the roots of her hair. Her hoarse, drawn-out cry startled her, even muffled by the expanse of his chest when she slumped forward.

Lost in her release, she vaguely felt his hands sliding over her sweat-slicked flesh. Then he clamped her lower body firmly down onto him, holding her still while he thrust strongly up. Seconds later she heard the air punch from his lungs and gush from his mouth. His arms slid up her back to wrap her up and cradle her against him. The sweat cooled on her skin, surprising her—she didn't sweat, ever.

He made her sweat.

Seven

Eve lay mostly on her stomach facing him, one hand curled around his upper arm. Her hair felt cool on his shoulder, her breathing steady and light. She obviously had no qualms about falling asleep after some pretty torrid lovemaking.

Whereas, he had been lying here on his back, trying not to breathe, for an hour, no closer to sleep than before.

He had never brought a woman to stay here overnight. Hotel rooms or unfamiliar feminine surroundings made him uncomfortable enough to leave before the morning light, albeit with grace and good manners.

He flexed his ankles. The tiny movement must have disturbed her, for she shifted, only a couple of inches but it was enough. With great care he slid from the bed.

Conn paced his dining room, feeling put out yet angry with himself for being away from her. Enthralling images of their lovemaking crept up on him in the dark and he shivered. She was a generous lover, experienced enough to give and take while he was bordering on a maniacal explosive desperation.

Generous, and easy to be with. What you saw was what you got with Eve. Joy and warmth. No embarrassment or self-consciousness. More passion than he had ever known, or elicited. He'd tried to outdo her but she matched him stroke for stroke, breath into breath. Hour for hour.

He yawned suddenly and widely. So why couldn't he just sleep with her?

Choosing a plump orange from the fruit bowl on the table, he peeled it while standing naked at the table, opening one of the many files that sat there. Seeing only her face.

After their first bout of loving, she'd teased him gently, made the smart-ass comment that if he ever got bored with construction, there was probably a porn movie production company somewhere that would be interested.

Conn smiled down at his files, shaking his head. She said the darnedest things. He liked that, the aftermath of sex being traditionally an uncomfortable time for him. Not that he'd had time to get uncomfortable. It was right about then she'd told him it was his turn to scream, and taken him in her hands.

He closed the file. Hopefully now that the overwhelming desire for her had been slaked—over and over—things would return to normal. He could get his mind back on the job.

He wandered back to his room, curious about her, and more than curious about her effect on him. She was still in the middle of the bed, slightly more on his side. He sat on the edge and finished the fruit, relishing the spurt of juice down his parched throat. Her face was on its side, tumbled

hair covering most of it. Her mouth was a soft plumped up
O where it pressed into the mattress. Elegant fingers spread
wide on his pillow.

Didn't she know it was his side she encroached on? His
pillow she clutched?

He smiled and then shivered again with an uneasy sense
of the tenderness that she evoked in him. She had looked
into his eyes and seen him as he used to be—why hadn't
she shied from it?

Then she moved, startling him. With a contented
"Mmmm," she rolled away from his side. One foot
escaped the duvet on the edge, peeking out. Her hands
were tucked into her chest. The sheet slid down her back,
leaving her shoulders bare and the tantalizing curve of her
rump disappearing under the crisp linen.

Okay, he had his side back. Work, or try for some sleep
before sunup?

The long line of her spine enticed him. He slid in stiffly,
taking care not to touch her.

A long time went by while Conn's breathing slowly
settled to a rhythm. His eyes were just beginning to drift
closed when Eve turned again with a restless flailing of
limbs and jammed back into his side.

He sighed carefully. Great.

Eve came awake slowly, aware of the lightness of the
room compared to hers. Immediately an exhilaration filled
her lungs, one of those rare, special-occasion thrills, like
Christmas or birthdays when she was little. Her wedding
day. Discovering she was pregnant.

The exhilaration that Conn brought to her.

And then came a sharp stab of disappointment that she

was alone. She reached out her hand and touched the place where he had lain spooned into her back, softly snoring in her ear.

What did she expect? He wasn't going to come quietly, her taciturn neighbor. A few hours wasn't going to be enough.

She snorted and buried her face in the pillow. Come quietly. He had started out that way but he was learning to let go. She'd told him he was too quiet to make up for the fact that she'd crowed her pleasure loud and long. "It's not as if the neighbors will mind."

She rolled onto her back, her good mood returning. Eve thought sex with her ex had been the most fun a person could have, but that had been a game, a dance. Any talking, any feeling had taken place outside the bed.

Conn was intense. So intense it was almost scary, which did sort of add to the excitement. His size floored her, the power in him that could break her in two, yet he wielded his limbs, his weight, his sex skillfully, so as not to hurt her.

But his intensity threw down a challenge. She refused to be some ritual that she suspected he went through every few months to make himself feel normal, human. Something to be dealt with, then forgotten. Eve didn't want him to forget ever.

As the minutes hurtled into hours, piece by piece of him had been stripped away. More and more he'd responded to her warmth, welcomed and reciprocated her touch. Once, feeling deliciously sated, she had covered his face with kisses, watching two little lines appear between his eyes in a perplexed frown.

"Look at you," she'd said. "All stern and composed."

It had taken a few seconds but eventually his mouth had twitched. "I'm smiling on the inside," he told her gravely.

And she remembered with a little thrill when she lay with her head on his chest, his hand on her hair. Eve had teased him about something or other and yes, there was hesitation—long seconds of it—but then, his hand moved jerkily and his fingers stroked through her hair. She'd known the warmth was there, the caring hidden under a decade of carefully constructed walls. This man had known love and laughter once, only he'd forced them down into a compartment named Distant Memories.

She wasn't going to be one of them.

Eve threw back the covers and bounded out of bed. Their clothes were piled on the elegant leather chaise by the window. Conn's dress shirt was on top, so she shoved her arms into it and ran her hands through her hair. She was still fastening buttons when she walked into the kitchen to see him standing by the window, looking out at her house. He wore trousers but no shirt. He glanced at her briefly, then more pointedly at his shirt before resuming his inspection of the countryside.

Even though he hadn't smiled, Eve didn't hesitate. She walked up behind him and slid her arms around his waist. And tried not to be hurt by the definite flinch of his skin.

"Sorry." Although she apologized, she made no effort to draw away.

Conn exhaled very slowly.

"Just takes a bit of getting used to," she murmured, burying her face in his tense back. "Touching."

He covered her hands with his and let his head loll back to rest on hers. She sighed with pleasure. It would be all right as long as she didn't push too hard.

"There is a car at your gate."

She tensed. All the events of last night, before Conn had

opened his door, came crashing back. And along with them, a double measure of guilt. She should have told him.

Eve slowly drew her arms away and stepped back. Damn Pete Scanlon to put a downer on the morning after a life-altering night.

Life altering for Eve. She couldn't speak for Conn.

He glanced at her, obviously expecting more interest in the car than she had displayed.

"I, uh, have to tell you something. Got any coffee?"

He tilted his head toward the kitchen and followed, handing her cups, leaning on the kitchen counter watching her pour.

"I didn't come over here last night to—" She couldn't help it, she could feel the color staining her cheeks. "I mean, I'm very glad we, uh—"

She pushed a full cup toward him and raised her own, hiding her face.

"Spit it out, Eve," Conn said, sounding amused. An almost smile brightened his eyes as they swept over her body. "It's not like you to be shy."

She might be relatively uninhibited in bed, but right this minute she felt ludicrous in his long white shirt, the tails flapping around her bare thighs.

She shuffled around and put the kitchen counter between them. Took in a deep breath. "Pete Scanlon's finished. It was on the news last night after you dropped me off."

He put his cup down slowly.

"He's being investigated for tax evasion and blackmail."

"Charges?"

Eve shook her head. "Not as of last night."

She outlined the details while he listened in silence, a grim look on his face.

Pete Scanlon's demise might be great news for Eve and for this city but it would have dire consequences for Conn's stadium.

When she finished, he tilted his head at the window. "What's the car outside your house got to do with it?"

"Oh, that arrived when I was on my way up here." She flicked a glance at the silvery car outside her gate. "I'd say it's a reporter. There were heaps of messages, all wanting a scoop. I'm afraid I figured quite heavily in the fallout on TV."

"He's been there since last night?"

Together they walked over to the window just as the car began moving up the hill toward them. Conn grabbed his keys from the fruit bowl and turned to the door but then stopped, scrutinizing her. She jumped when he suddenly reached out and began undoing buttons. With his eyes boring into hers, her heartbeat was the only part of her capable of reacting. She stood captivated by his gaze, which seemed to be daring her to cover herself or protest. The shirt open, he slid it down her shoulders and arms and, still watching her, donned it himself.

Eve stood straight and tall, her heart pounding, willing him to touch her, to do whatever he wanted. What was the point in being self-conscious when she had displayed every inch of herself to him last night.

He buttoned up the shirt, still watching her. "The room suits you," he murmured finally then turned away.

And the moment his eyes left hers, the spell was broken. The realization that she stood naked in a glass palace in the cold light of day with a stranger approaching, hit her like a high-pressure blast of cold water. The second she heard the door close behind him, Eve scooted down the hall to the safety of his bedroom, fervently hoping that the little winking cubes in every corner of every room were security sensors and not CCTV.

Throwing her clothes on, she crept to the bedroom window and peeked out. The remote-controlled security gates were scraping closed as the strange car pulled up outside. Conn moved into view, stopping inside the gates, and conversed with the driver through his wound-down window.

"You were right," he told her a couple of minutes later, a brief sardonic lift of his brows the only sign that he found her self-consciousness amusing.

She studied the business card he handed her. It was the man from the television station who had called last night.

"I told him you had gone into town for a few days to stay with friends."

She sighed, sitting down. "I suppose I'll have to speak to them at some stage. I really don't want this to be about my being fired. Scanlon has so much else to answer for."

"You started the ball rolling. You're in it up to your neck."

To her ears, it sounded like an accusation. "Do you blame me?" she asked defensively.

Conn's lips thinned, but he shook his head.

The bubble of hurt subsided. This was a difficult situation for both of them. Again she silently cursed Pete Scanlon. Would she never be free of him? "I'm sorry. I should have told you last night."

Conn gave a short bark of laughter. "I didn't exactly give you much of a chance." He clasped his hands together and cupped them at the back of his head. "I'd made up my mind about ten seconds before you rang the bell. If you hadn't come to me, I was coming to you, cursing myself for being every kind of weak fool." He paused. "But I'm not sorry for it."

Eve hugged herself, breathing out in relief. He wasn't sorry for it. Thank you, God.

But would he be sorry eventually? The pleasure of his admission faded. "That reporter will think it strange you'd know my whereabouts."

Conn moved into the kitchen and raised the coffee pot. "We're neighbors in an isolated area. It's natural we would watch each other's properties when the other was away."

She shook her head no to the offer of coffee. "How do we handle this? If they find out we—know each other, you'll be implicated, too."

Conn put the pot down carefully. "If they find out we're sleeping together, you mean."

"This could put you in the spotlight. And maybe more would come out than just your contributions to the campaign."

Conn inhaled, understanding turning his eyes bleak. "The accident. Rachel." He rubbed his face. "It'll be so much more fun now that I'm successful. The vultures will enjoy cutting me down, especially as I've turned down every invitation to be interviewed over the years."

This glimpse of his private pain lanced through her. She should get away from here, not be seen with him. Eve couldn't bear to be the instrument of his humiliation. "I should go." She stood up, ineffectually smoothing her wrinkled skirt. "Before they tie us together."

He threw her an admonitory look. "There were reporters in droves at the fund-raiser last night. I don't know if any of them saw our little tête-à-tête with Scanlon, but they definitely saw you and me together." He cleared his throat. "And then there was the kiss."

Eve felt a little bruise of hurt. His lack of protest suggested he did not want to be connected to her—except in the privacy of his home.

He glanced back out the window and frowned. "There are now two cars outside your house." The search of a kitchen drawer produced a pair of binoculars. "Same silver one as before and a green one. They're talking to each other."

Conn handed Eve the binoculars. She did not recognize either of the men leaning against their cars chatting, their faces toward her house.

What were they to do? Her presence here was bad for his reputation. "I could get on the floor of your car, covered up with something." She was only half joking.

"Ashamed, Eve?"

His face was impenetrable, giving her no clue as to what he meant.

"Conn, I'm not ashamed to be with you. Quite the opposite."

Conn turned back to the window. "And now a third car." His hand tapped his thigh. "We haven't done anything illegal. Why should you sneak out of my house like a criminal?"

"Being seen with me is going to cause you—and your parents—more hassle. I hate that."

He faced her and put his hands on the kitchen counter between them. "Then stay here."

Her head shot up.

"Stay here," Conn repeated. "They can't get in past my security gates. And unless they're on a boat, with a powerfully long lens, or they manage to climb the cliff, they can't see us. No one can see us unless we go out the back of the house."

What crazy warm feeling was this suffusing her at this

ridiculous idea? She was supposed to be thinking of a way to distance herself to avoid causing him more pain. "Don't you have to work?" she asked faintly.

He nodded.

"How can I stay here? I have no other clothes."

Conn leaned forward on the counter, using those body-builder shoulders to brace himself, and cast his eyes slowly, thoroughly, over every inch of her. Her chest expanded as memories of that same pose, only with her under him, ignited what could only be described as a hot flash—and she was *way* too young to be suffering those.

"So?"

Oh, and he'd used that tone, sultry, commanding, impossible to deny…

So fast her head spun, she was awash with a shivery desire. He made her sweat, made every muscle tighten in anticipation. Pushed all the buttons she had. Was this normal or even healthy? He was like an invasion, filling her with reckless sensual energy.

Big bad Connor Bannerman was completely irresistible.

"Or I could be—" his voice was as close to a growl as she'd ever heard, and his teeth flashed briefly "—*nice,* and have my secretary bring you some things from town."

Eve slumped when his smoldering eyes released her from their hold. He had made his decision. Evidently no input from her was required, even if she was incapable of speech. "We'll hole up till they leave."

He picked up his phone and dialed. She listened to him telling someone called Phil to purchase woman's underclothing and T-shirts, a pair of jeans. He raised his eyebrows at her to see if she concurred with his order and the sizes he guessed at. There was a discussion of toiletries and food as well.

Eve turned to the window, still overheated. She had half expected him to leap the counter between them and take her where she stood. Such was the power of his proprietary, scorching look.

She was half disappointed he hadn't.

Her heart still at a canter, she looked out at the stupendous view. He was right. No one could see them here at the front of the house, unless they were on a boat and had binoculars or a powerful camera. It would be completely private.

She cast a furtive look in Conn's direction as the phone conversation turned to work matters. He stood at the table, the phone to his ear, opening his laptop.

It was ridiculous for him to expect her to stay here, a prisoner in his house until the heat was off.

Eve turned back to the window, feeling faint with unabated desire. Here, with him, alone. For days, maybe. She should have stopped him.

Why didn't she?

Later that afternoon they heard the beep of his secretary's car at his gate. Eve got up from where she had been reading on the couch, thinking it prudent to disappear. She peeked out of Conn's bedroom window, watching him help a middle-aged woman with several shopping bags. Both of them disappeared inside. She looked down the hill to see the three cars still sitting at her gate.

Eve decided to take a bath. Conn's bathroom was out of this world. Easily as big as her living room at home, with an oversize and open shower and a huge round bath with spa operation. Big, like everything else in this house, including its owner.

She had a leisurely soak, then dwarfed herself in the folds of his expensive robe and fell asleep on his great big bed. When she awoke, the shopping bags were at the end of the bed and the coverlet was turned up over her. She rummaged in the bags and dressed in jeans that fit perfectly and a long-sleeved tee that was huge. The underwear wasn't exactly what she would have chosen but it made her smile to think he'd bought them for her.

When she went downstairs, he was sitting alone at the table, immersed in work. Eve hated to disturb him, feeling somewhat responsible for the trouble she had caused. "Would you mind if I explored the house?"

Conn waved a hand, barely looking up.

She ventured down some stairs off the kitchen and walked into a wine cellar that would hold a couple of hundred bottles, she calculated, far surpassing the wine collection she and James had taken such pride in. Next she discovered another huge bedroom and bathroom and a separate, more-formal lounge that was probably never used. There was an impressive gym—naturally—and indoor pool at the back of the house.

Another surprise, the entire left wing of the house held two fully self-contained units, each with its own spa on a private deck in front. The king-size beds were not made up, but the rooms were richly furnished.

After an hour wandering around, touching the beautiful fittings and admiring the view, Eve headed back to the main house, more than a little curious. What on earth could the man want with holiday accommodations and a professional wine cellar?

Conn was in the kitchen, fixing a salad to go with two fat steaks he had set aside. Eve's stomach reminded her she hadn't eaten since their late breakfast. She set the table while he broiled the steaks.

As they ate, she asked him about the units.

"When I built the place, I had no intention of staying. It was to be sold as a retreat. Exclusive bed and breakfast accommodation with a restaurant."

Hence the wine cellar, Eve thought. "But you liked it."

"I liked it very much."

"You could still do that. It's big enough that you could still have your own space."

He looked up from his plate, his mouth curved in a wry smile. "You mean, should I suffer a cataclysmic event and suddenly feel the need to have people around?"

Eve set her fork down, feeling reckless even as she cautioned herself. She couldn't let that remark go. One day her confidence in human nature was going to get her heart broken—again. "Am I people, Conn?"

That stalled him. Eve's insides shivered deliciously. She was learning to read his eyes, the brooding mouth. What perplexed her was the surprise in his voice when he eventually answered her.

"No-o," he said, drawing the syllable out. "You're Eve."

Eight

"How did it go?" Eve met him at the door, waiting while he shed his overcoat. Conn's face was lined with worry. He'd just returned from his "Please Explain" meeting with his board of directors.

"As I expected."

They walked down the hallway, Conn looking sideways at her.

Eve wore a sage-colored jersey and long black peasant skirt. Her face was made up for the first time in days and her hair pulled back in a short single plait.

"You've been home," was his only comment.

Both of them had noticed yesterday that there were no cars outside Eve's gate. Neither mentioned that the heat was off and there was no real need for her to stay here with him. Her going back to her house today proved that nothing was forever, that reality was upon them. That each led different, separate lives.

Eve had been cooking. The kitchen was rich with the aroma of chicken and sage. "Tell me about it."

The board had insisted Conn prove that the contributions to Scanlon's campaign were the only business dealings he had with the disgraced man. They were satisfied that all accounts were in order and all contributions documented.

As they ate, he told her it was less simple to come up with an idea to sell them on raising Bannerman, Inc.'s stake in the stadium. He had managed to add to the list of sponsors, as well as increase existing contributions. But the mayor was adamant that too much public money was still being poured into the project. Money that the council didn't have.

"A decade ago when New Zealand bid for the World Cup, the council was on the verge of an election. They gave an assurance that they would back the stadium to forty percent. Whoever won the tender would do the rest."

Over the years, ensuing councils invested heavily in a scheme to build a ring road to ease traffic flow. But recently there had been a massive property boom. The council's commitment to buy up the houses on land destined for the road was in trouble.

"The mayor hadn't budgeted for that," Conn explained. "Benson's well over budget for the road and is trying to wheedle out of the commitment to the stadium. Admitting the blunder will lose them this election, even with Scanlon out of the picture."

"But surely Benson knows he has to back the stadium to ensure public votes."

"He's not going to broadcast his opposition, not with the election a little over a week away," Conn conceded. "But he's stalling. The money isn't forthcoming, the building is being held up. They're hoping we'll just suck it up and finance the whole thing."

"So what can you do?" Eve asked. The World Cup was less than two years away. Conn needed every minute of that to complete the stadium, but with the council reneging on the finance, and the day to day inspections and consents, he was going to run out of time.

Conn told her he'd gone head to head with his board of directors and they had finally agreed to sell one of the company's South Island forests. He had also persuaded them to withdraw their tender to build a hotel chain in the South Pacific. However, both options were subject to a vote in a shareholders meeting to be held in two days.

"The board is with you, then?" Eve stood and cleared the empty plates. She felt at home in his house, and Conn seemed less distant, tolerant of her music and more talkative. They shared similar philosophies of society and politics. He even smiled sometimes, a real smile that reached his eyes.

And the simmering desire between them was always just below the surface, threatening—often succeeding—to overwhelm them in the middle of any activity. In the past few days, there had been dinners burned, drinks spilled, clothing scattered all over the floor, when their passion swept them away.

"It's not unanimous," Conn told her. "There are one or two on the board who'll have my head on a platter if it doesn't work out. We spent a lot of time and money preparing the bid for the hotel chain. If I hadn't managed to get the new sponsors on board, I doubt we would have had an agreement."

"Will it be enough?"

He shook his head, looking grim. "It's a goodwill gesture, that's all. Somehow the mayor has to be shamed into fulfilling his side of the bargain."

Eve suppressed a smile. Her thoughts exactly!

She finished her preparations and picked up a lavishly decorated cake, her stomach tight with anticipation. Conn looked up, the surprise in his face as bright and sharp as the flickering candles.

"Da-da!" She placed the cake in front of him with a flourish then bent to kiss his astonished mouth. "Happy birthday."

"How…?"

"Your mother phoned—don't worry, I didn't answer," she added quickly. "I was in the lounge when the phone rang so I heard her message. Which said something like 'Happy birthday, love. Come by soon.'"

She turned her attention back to the cake. "It's pineapple and brazil nut cake. Make a wish and blow out the candles."

Conn looked at her as if she was speaking Swahili. Sighing, she picked up the cake cutter and put it in his hand. Placing her hand on his cheek, she turned his head gently to the front so he was looking at her masterpiece.

"You made this?"

Eve nodded and stood over him until he eventually leaned toward the glittering cake and blew out the candles. She clapped her hands and moved back to her seat. "I hope you made a wish."

Conn stared down at the cake. "You have hidden talents."

Eve picked up her wine and sipped. "You'd better believe it." Then she leaned forward, her hands clasped in front of her.

JAN COLLEY 119

Conn looked at her and gave a weak smile. "You look like you're about to read the news."

"Since you mentioned it, I've been on the phone all day. Apparently I'm a hero since Grant's admission. They're bending over backward to get me back."

Eve outlined her plan. She wanted to front a hastily put-together TV special to air the day after tomorrow, one week before the election. She'd gotten a verbal assurance for thirty minutes prime time and was hoping the station would give her an hour. "We'll interview people on the street, small-town grass-roots rugby communities. See how they feel about the world cup being run here. Get some former national players on the show, the tourism minister. And if I get the second half hour, there would be a poll— live to air—to gauge support for the stadium. People could call in, e-mail, text—like *Pop Idol*."

Eve had used such techniques before to gauge public opinion. It was simple and effective. It made politics popular.

"The good news is, I heard today that less than ten percent of the votes have been returned so far." While governmental elections had polling stations, local body elections were generally conducted by postal vote. "That means we can work on all those people who have yet to send their votes in."

Conn gazed at her, his smile more circumspect. "Congratulations. You've got your job back."

Eve shook her head. "This is just a one-off."

He picked up his glass. "I doubt that. You were made for TV, Eve."

He clearly wasn't as excited as she'd hoped. "I'm not thinking past the election. What do you think?"

"Scanlon's gone. Your father is avenged. What's in this for you?"

Eve blanched. How could he even ask? Was it so hard for him to believe that she would want to do something for him, just because it was him? "Use your initiative, Conn," she said quietly. Because I made things worse for you. Because I don't want you to fail. Because I'm crazy about you.

Something in her face must have unnerved him, because he looked away, rubbing his chin. "It's not the way I do things. I have a PR team that deals with the media."

"Use me, Conn. Like it or not, people listen to me. They watch me."

Picking up the slice, he cut into the cake with steely concentration.

"Pete's gone," she continued, "and he was by far the front-runner for this election. But there are other candidates. Benson has to see his position is still under threat. If he ignores the support for the stadium, he will lose votes big-time."

Conn stood and brought her a generous slice of cake. "I'll talk to my people tomorrow. See what they think."

Eve wasn't going to let him away with that. "I need an answer tonight. We'll have to start taping tomorrow to set this up in time."

He responded with a tight nod. "I'll think about it."

"Give me the sponsors' names. They love publicity. I would also like to tour the site, on camera. Show the progress you've made."

He took a forkful of cake, not looking at her.

"And—" she swallowed…might as well get it over with "—I want you."

Conn stilled, midchew.

Eve waited nervously. She would do the show without him, but for human impact, he would be a definite bonus.

"Right this very minute?" he asked, deceptively light.

"On the show, Conn."

His incredulous eyes lashed her face. "You can't be serious." He might as well have said, "Over my dead body."

Eve rose, dragging her chair close to his. "Just for a few minutes." She put a hand gently on his thigh. "You can approve the script. If you prefer not to be in a formal interview situation, then why not conduct the tour? Show people your stadium, like you showed me."

His laugh was bitter. "Eve, the kind of publicity I can bring this project is the very worst kind. You want one way to kill this thing dead, you just thought of it."

Eve shook her head. "*I'm* interviewing you, no one else. After this, you go back to how you normally handle your press."

Conn stood and picked up his plate. "That would be a no," he said flatly, turning his back on her to walk into the kitchen.

She jumped up and followed with a determined step. "Conn, it's time to let the past go."

"Being plastered all over the TV and newspapers is only going to bring it back. Christ, Eve—" he turned to glare at her "—Think of how her parents will feel, seeing my face again."

"Do you really think, after all this time, they are still going to blame you?"

"Of course they will," he told her in a bitter voice. "She was twenty-one years old. She had her whole life taken away from her. Think of how you would feel if someone ripped your child away."

It was like a physical blow to her stomach. She felt the color leech out of her face and might have buckled if her hands had not been resting on the kitchen counter.

"Do what you want," Conn turned back to the sink. "Leave me out of it."

Eve took a couple of brittle steps to the table, exhaling carefully. She'd thought she was over this gut-wrenching pain, the pain that struck when she was usually alone, not doing anything special. It always surprised her how much it hurt.

She had never been a crier, but these last few weeks she had shed more tears—over her father's death, her divorce and the baby that would never leave her heart—than she had in her lifetime. That's what you get for neglecting your hurts all your life.

Please don't let me cry. Don't let him see me cry. Conn Bannerman wouldn't understand tears. He had spent a lifetime covering up his pain and needed no one to help him cope with his tragic memories. He would be scathing in the face of her weakness.

Her fingers gripped the table so hard, she felt her fingernails bend back. The cringing pain in her heart set her knees trembling with the effort required not to curl over and hug herself. Hug her baby to her. Hold it there, always.

Then she felt his hands, gentle on her shoulders.

"Hey, hey," he murmured, his hands rubbing and soothing. "I'm sorry I snapped. I know you're only trying to help."

He turned her in his arms and smoothed her hair back while she pressed her face into his shirt, embarrassed. Conn pulled her down with him onto the sofa. Her back was to him and he wrapped his arms around her middle, holding her close. "I do appreciate what you're trying to do."

She sniffed. "I hate crying." Her hand swiped at the tears that spilled over. "It just takes me over sometimes." She looked down at his arm around her waist and twisted his watch strap. "Lately, a lot of things are taking me by surprise."

He kissed her hair. "It surprised you that I said no?"

What surprised her was his gentleness. She'd discovered he could be gentle even in the most violent passion. But the caring man holding her, wiping her tears away, was unexpected. "I've always been good at putting on a brave face. Concentrating on work and not letting things get me down. But since I stopped work, everything seems to have caught me up." She sighed, and it was such a sad sound her tears started up again. "I had a miscarriage before I came back home."

She heard a softly uttered curse. Guilt, no doubt, at his comment a couple of minutes ago. His hands stroked her hair and he pulled her head back on his shoulder.

Eve told him haltingly how she fell pregnant when she and her husband made up after she discovered his infidelity.

"Was that why you came home?"

Eve nodded. She was half sitting, half lying in his arms. Slowly his hand moved down her front, over her breasts and stopped just under her rib cage. She looked down. His large hand covered virtually her entire abdomen. It was utterly, shockingly intimate to feel his warm fingers spread wide on her belly, as if he could protect what had been there. The warmth of it soothed the cold ache within.

"I'm so scared I won't be able to…" The tears started up again and he pressed gently down. Eve placed her hand over top of his. If only he had been the father. Instinctively Eve knew that Conn would protect their baby with his life, as he eased her ache now.

I'm in love with him, she thought with wonder, squeezing her eyes shut. Because I'm needy and hurt and I can see his baby in this little scene, as if I'm up there in another world looking down. Because I'm strong and can warm his cold bones and cold heart.

Because he will never touch another woman like he is touching me now.

"That's why it's all caught up with you now," he was saying, and his voice was so gentle it curled around her pain like a caress. "You've stopped your crazy schedule and have time to think about things."

Too caught up in the realization that she loved him, Eve could not reply.

He pressed another kiss to the top of her head, and she wriggled in closer. It was every girl's dream to be wrapped up in a big man's arms, to have this feeling of being enveloped in safety and caring. That's why we do it, she thought. Why we give in too soon to attraction and hang on too long after the attraction is gone. It's not that we're weak. It's that being nurtured feeds us, strengthens our own female need to nurture.

Women are easy. Why didn't men get that? Who would have thought this man, with all his tragic, self-imposed exile from the world would listen and cuddle?

Hope nearly swamped her. Maybe she *was* the one who could reconcile him to rejoin the living, instead of sitting in the dark with his silent ghosts.

He shifted under her. "I'll do it."

Eve gave another loud sniff and twisted around to look at him.

"The TV show."

She searched his face, and her hope died a little. He was miles away. Not here with her, touching the life that was. With something or someone else.

Rachel?

"Feeling sorry for me, Conn?" she asked, a tightness in her throat.

"No." He shook his head. "Because I want this stadium to be built." He paused, and his hand pressed briefly down again on her stomach. "For my father."

"Your father?"

"It's always been his dream to see the World Cup here. Maybe if I succeed, it will make up for...everything."

Of course. The stadium to ease the pain of a disappointed father. In his eyes, anyway. "You won't regret it," she whispered.

Conn pushed her up and slid out from under her. His mouth twisted. "Oh, I expect I will."

Nine

Eve left early next morning for a full day at the television station. She called Conn to say she had been granted the second half hour and was off to interview the minister of tourism, who was passing through the airport. Reporters were talking to the public everywhere, discussing the upcoming World Cup and what the stadium meant to them.

Conn met her at the stadium midafternoon. She had earlier faxed a list of questions for his approval but for the most part it was a casual walkabout and the taping went without a hitch.

The next day they would tape the live part of the show and open the lines to the public. Conn declined her invitation to watch from the station as the shareholders meeting was scheduled for that afternoon. But he surprised them both when he offered to drive her to the terminal.

They drew up to the wharf, and Conn turned off the

ignition. The ferry from the city had just docked. Eve gathered up her hold-all and briefcase and they sat silent for a minute.

He stared straight ahead, unable to express his gratitude for what she was doing for him, yet frustrated that it was necessary. He preferred to fight his own battles. "The irony of this isn't lost on me," he said quietly. "I have spent what seems like a lifetime hating people like you. TV people, reporters…and now I'm using you—your face, your name—to help my cause."

Eve leaned toward him and put her hand on his cheek.

"It was my idea, Conn. I want to do it and I think it will work. The stadium is the important thing here, right?"

Too generous by far, he thought, watching her go. Here they were, united, fighting the good fight. But what would happen when this was over?

On the way home he called in to the small convenience store on the edge of the village. His housekeeper did his grocery shopping, but having two people in the house meant supplies were dwindling.

He picked up a basket at the front of the store, not quite sure what he was looking for. The least he could do was fix Eve a nice supper when she came home tonight.

When she came home… When had his home become her home? His mind skipped around the thought that he liked having her there. The first day or so he'd retreated to his office when he wanted to work but found he kept staring at the door, wondering what she was up to. So he had taken to working in his usual spot at the dining table. One day, she looked up from preparing food and caught him staring at her.

"Sorry, I was humming again, wasn't I?"

The truth was it had been an effortless slide into wanting

to see her and listen to her. Doing his best not to smile at her often zany humor. Even her chatter and incessant music didn't bug him as it should.

He inspected the rather motley array of salad vegetables, thinking this was the last thing he'd expected. It was the novelty of it. Having someone else around. Sharing.

The lady at the checkout swiped his card and then said casually, "That's a nice picture of you and Eve Summers in *Women's Weekly*."

Conn blinked at her and she pointed to a stack of magazines on the counter.

The night of the fund-raiser. The headline emblazoned across the cover was "Eve's Favorite Subject."

It *was* a nice picture—of her. She smiled right into the lens, the consummate professional. That suit really was a piece of work. However, Conn spoiled it with his thunderous scowl. No one would guess the iron grip she had on his arm as she propelled him away. *"Just walk."*

"Eve is my favorite person on TV." The woman beamed, pushing his purchases toward him.

Conn smiled tightly. "Mine, too," he muttered, stalking out before he did something stupid like buy the damn thing. He burned to know if the kissing photo was in there.

Driving home, he told himself that of course people were going to notice their relationship. She was a celebrity. It went with the territory.

Whereas he liked his solitude. What need did he have of intimacy and domesticity?

Which reminded him. Setting the groceries on the table, he picked up the phone and dialed his parents' number. "Mum? Eve is doing a thing on TV tonight. Thought you guys might like to watch it."

His mother was ecstatic, which made him smile. Maybe one day he could forge a better, closer relationship with his parents—his mother, anyway. As long as she didn't take to trying to matchmake all the time like she did in the years after the accident. She had to know there weren't going to be big weddings and happy families where he was concerned. His sister, Erin, was doing admirably in that department.

Conn organized supper, then settled down to some last-minute paperwork. The shareholders were the next hurdle, and his presentation would have to be spectacular to sway them. Pity the meeting was not tomorrow; Eve's TV special may have been good for a few votes.

Later that day he presided at the hastily called gathering. His two-man PR team sat stiffly, usurped of their usual role of heading these meetings and fronting for the media, of which there was a sizable contingent.

Conn took care to conceal his distaste at being in the limelight and made a compelling case for selling the South Island forest in order to pour more money into the stadium. The postponement of the South Pacific hotel chain created some opposition, but in the end the shareholders were almost unanimous in their support. Even the media crush at the end was not too odious. Conn was surprised to find that business reporters stuck pretty well to business facts.

Now there was nothing further to do but watch Eve's special and wait for the election.

Eve let herself into the house and raced down the hallway, unable to contain her excitement. The silence was a dash of cold water. So was the sight of Conn Bannerman sitting at the table, up to his elbows in papers.

He looked up as she skidded to a halt, her eyes moving

from his face to the dark and silent television screen across the large room. "Did you watch?"

Conn leaned back in his seat, a perplexed line between his eyes. "Watch what?"

Deflated, she stared at him until finally his mouth twitched in one corner. The delight bubbled up again and she launched herself at him.

Conn rose to meet her, his smile as wide as the arms that stretched out to catch her and sweep her up.

"We did it!" Eve crowed, twining her arms around his neck and holding on as her feet sailed around in nearly a full circle.

"*You* did it." He planted a wide smacking kiss on her lips. "You were brilliant."

"Oh! It was so great. Even I had no idea…ninety-two percent! Can you believe it?"

Ninety-two percent support. Eve decided ninety-two was going to be her lucky number from now on.

Support for the Gulf Harbor Stadium was overwhelming. According to her television special, everyone from Bluff in the deep south to Kataia in the far north wanted the World Cup to be held here. And they wanted the mayor of their largest city to uphold his commitment to it, even though that commitment had been made by a different mayor years ago.

"The news will be on." She broke away and rushed across to the other side of the room, grabbing the remote on the way. Conn went to the kitchen to get the champagne from the fridge.

Pete Scanlon being charged with blackmail and drug-related offences led the bulletin. More charges were expected to follow when the Serious Fraud Office had completed its investigations. He was granted bail but was required to hand over his passport.

Over, she thought. Old news. Now that he had his come-uppance, and, there was an easing to some extent of her pain about the last few unhappy years of her father's life, Pete Scanlon did not interest her.

Eve's special was the second item. Engrossed, she backed slowly to the huge leather couch, barely noticing when Conn handed her a fizzing flute. "'Unprecedented.'" She quoted the broadcaster's words. Out of the corner of her eye, she saw Conn raise his glass. "'An amazing comeback…'" Absently she raised her glass and clinked his. "Look, and there you are." She turned and beamed at him and they sat down on the couch together. "You have a great face for the camera, Mr. Bannerman."

Conn raised his brows and kept his eyes on the television.

"'Thrown the gauntlet to Mayor Benson…' oh, this is great stuff," Eve enthused. "He now has to show his hand, one way or the other—and soon."

"A week to the election…" Conn began, his glass halfway to his lips.

The object of his attention was on screen now, shaking his head at the camera. "I'm rather busy to be spending my time in front of the television…no doubt it will be in the papers tomorrow…" Mayor Benson said in response to an inquiry about seeing Eve's special. "Bannerman, Inc. and this council have a very good relationship…" he said in response to what he thought about claims that the council was reneging on financial and procedural commitments. "Of course the Gulf Harbor Stadium would be a valuable asset to this city. We also have other considerations—transport, for instance." The mayor waved all other questions aside and went determinedly back to the safety of the black tie dinner he was attending.

"What now?" Eve turned to Conn.

He sipped and swallowed. "I think we'll go see him tomorrow. My people have presented the offer my board has made to reduce the amount of public monies, so I would like some feedback on that. I want to hear him say to my face that he cocked up his budget and can't afford to uphold his end of our bargain. But I'd like to see you two go head-to-head also. Mayor Benson has about as much liking for the media as I do."

Eve tilted her head and fluttered her lashes with tragic comedy. "Still?"

Conn's eyes settled on her face, shining with admiration. Oh, Eve wanted to hold this moment forever. She'd done well. He was very pleased, even if he wasn't the type to laugh out loud or shout it from the rooftops. His quiet approval was all she needed.

Her mind was so full of him—how sexy and handsome and serious he was. How he'd driven her this morning. Admitted his gratitude. Bought champagne…she almost missed the newsreader's next words. Alerted by the beetling of Conn's brow, she turned back to the screen.

"Speculation is growing that there is more to the relationship between construction magnate, Connor Bannerman, and Eve Drumm, the popular presenter of tonight's TV special on the Gulf Harbor Stadium."

There was a clip of Conn and her walking around the stadium, filming his progress.

"It would be an unlikely pairing, given their opposing political views. Bannerman was a staunch supporter of

Pete Scanlon's mayoral campaign, while Eve was instrumental in bringing him down."

The camera showed the cover of *Women's Weekly* magazine, Eve and Conn leaving the theater the night of the fund-raiser.

"It seems being on opposite sides of the political fence," the newsreader droned on in a smug voice, "is no barrier to friendship."

So what? Eve thought, stealing a look at the magnate's face. As she feared, his lip was curled in a scowl.

"Blackmail, fraud—and Eve and Conn have a night on the town," he muttered.

Eve shrugged. "So?" She raised her glass. "Here's to us."

Conn set his glass down on the coffee table and leaned back. "He's right."

Eve's heart sank. The celebrations hadn't lasted nearly long enough.

"What *do* we have in common?"

His quiet question brought her another step further down. It was an effort to keep her voice light. "I think we do pretty well, don't we?"

"The social butterfly and the grouch."

No one could do brooding like Conn. "It's a start."

Eve knew they had accomplished what they set out to do—as long as the election results were in their favor. They had banded together in a common cause. He'd been supportive of her in regard to Pete Scanlon. She'd supported him with his stadium.

But there was more to this relationship than that, much more. And tonight was their night, their victory. He was not going to get away with spoiling that. Not while there was champagne…

She set her glass down next to his and leaned over him. "Let's see. You like my cooking. I like designer letterboxes." Her fingers walked up his chest, slow and seductive. With a deft flick, the first button popped. "I get all mushy when a guy—any guy—paints my bedroom. You like yelling at me and then kissing me." She nuzzled his neck. "I like your folks." Another button…and another. Her champagne-cooled tongue flicked the soft spot behind his earlobe at the same time the pads of her fingertips ran over his nipples. "And the way your body tenses when I do that."

She drew back to look at his face, her fingers making short work of the rest of his buttons.

Unsmiling, heavy-lidded, eyes darkening. Tension in his mouth. Oh, yeah, he was turned on all right.

Her fingers moved lower. "I love champagne."

His head rolled back when her hand slid under the waistband of his pants. That broad expanse of chest rose as he arched his back a little. She scraped the nails of her other hand down the steely ridges of his stomach and tugged on the fastening. "You will, too."

Conn swallowed, his eyes closing. "I—do…"

Eve eased his zip down smiling at the strain in his voice. His skin was already hot and stretched tight when she bared him. She closed her hand around him, or around as much of him as her average-size hand could. A strong pulse beat against her palm.

This would be interesting, a new experience for them. Her hand began to move, sliding up and down firmly. Conn's chest had risen higher, expanded as he filled his lungs with air. Eve worked him with one hand while reaching behind her for the glass of champagne with the other.

Just then he opened his eyes, his exhalation forgotten as he realized what she was about to do.

Holding his gaze, she took a mouthful of the wonderful foamy liquid and lowered her head. Watched his jaw clench and the thick column of his throat bulge and ripple in another hard swallow. The bubbles in her mouth boiled and hissed around his scorching flesh like the air that was forced between his lips.

She'd made her point, she thought later while clearing the lounge of not one but two empty champagne bottles. Conn was nothing if not fair minded. He'd absolutely insisted that they open another bottle: damn the expense, so long as he got to return the favor.

They did *so* have something in common. Eve chuckled as she turned off the lights and headed for the bedroom. They both loved champagne.

Ten

The following day, she accompanied him to his appointment with the mayor. With Eve as his secret weapon, Conn underlined the offer already tabled to up Bannerman, Inc.'s financial holding in the stadium. The media had made much of the fact that with less than a week till the election, little more than ten percent of the postal votes had been received. The mayor reluctantly agreed that it might be in his best interests to come out publicly in support of the Gulf Harbor Stadium in the limited time left before the election.

Eve and Conn exited the meeting hopeful, aware they had done all they could to secure the completion of Conn's project on time. The rest was up to the people of the city.

It was still early afternoon. "We deserve a treat," Eve declared, stopping a few meters away from Conn's chauffeured BMW. "Let's cut your driver loose and visit your parents."

Conn looked at his watch with a grimace. "It's an hour and a half drive."

"I'll drive." She patted his rear end playfully. "I've been dying to get my hands on your big grunty motor." She rounded the car to smile at the driver alighting. Conn stood on the other side of the car, frowning.

"Oh, come on, Conn," she wheedled. "It was your birthday the other day. I bet there'll be presents."

His sigh was heavy, but he reluctantly told his driver he had the rest of the day free.

His mother bubbled over with delight at the unexpected visit. Eve was welcomed like a cherished friend and helped Mrs. Bannerman with coffee and cake. The two men were quiet. Conn seemed to have ants in his pants. He prowled the room, examining objects and offering one-syllable answers to his mother's quick-fire questions.

"When was this taken?" He picked up a framed photo of a tall smiling woman holding two toddlers in her lap.

"A year ago. His sister, Erin," Mrs. Bannerman explained to Eve. "She is a year older."

Conn stared at the photo for a long time, then replaced it on the shelf. "She's put on weight."

"She was pregnant then, with Cinnamon."

"When did you last see her?" Eve asked. She'd thought it odd that aside from a phone call, none of his family had visited on his birthday. Her family traditionally made a big fuss of birthdays and Christmas.

Conn shrugged and rubbed the back of his neck. "I haven't seen Erin for, must be a couple of years." He resumed circling the room, unable to settle.

"Four years, dear," his mother chided. "You haven't

seen her since they moved up to the city." Again she turned to Eve. "Erin's husband is a policeman."

Eve was really shocked now. So Conn's sister lived right in the city where he worked, only a quick ferry ride away, and yet they hadn't seen each other in four years? What had happened to splinter this family so?

She watched the uncomfortable man pace the room as if it was a cell. How she wanted to ask, but that breached the propriety of politeness. She decided to distract Conn, put him more at ease. "I want to see your room." She set her cup and saucer down. Mrs. Bannerman jumped to her feet, Mr. Bannerman coughed and Conn Bannerman looked baffled.

His mother led the way. "Connor moved out of the house when he was thirteen, telling us he was old enough to live in the butler's house and look after himself. Not that it's a house, or we ever had a butler. It was just a name for the sleep-out in the backyard. Goodness knows what he used to get up to out here, he never invited us in."

The two women were well ahead of the men as Mrs. Bannerman pushed into a small unattached cabin under a tree in the big backyard. Eve wrinkled her nose as she stepped inside, not quite sure of the odor. It wasn't unpleasant, just unidentifiable.

But she forgot it when she saw the memorabilia covering every surface. There was host of framed portraits on the walls; Conn's rugby history, from age seven up.

He was easy to pick out. How could he be so good-looking all his life? She had been gangly, metal-mouthed, with long stringy hair, until she was at least thirteen or fourteen. Her family hadn't had the money for nice clothes or hairdressers back then.

But there had still been love, lots of love.

She moved to the dresser and examined more photos, family shots, many of the tall dark boy and his sister who looked almost like a twin. Every photograph showed him smiling. A petty and confusing jealousy twisted Eve's insides, for she knew what it was to have to work a smile out of him. Clearly, it hadn't always been so.

The two men finally stepped into the room. She stole a look at Conn's face. For a second his eyes lit up. There was a rugby ball sitting on the pillows of the single bed in the corner. He picked it up, weighed it in his hands.

"I wondered why your bedroom at home is so stark," she commented. "It's all here."

Too late she realized what she'd said, saw the lift of Conn's head. Oh, great! Talk about foot-in-mouth disease…

She risked a look at him. His brows rose slightly, but then Mrs. Bannerman gasped and they both turned to look at her. She glared at her husband, who coughed and looked at Conn. Eve swore there was a twinkle in his eye.

"Wondered where that got to," Mr. Bannerman muttered, scratching his head. She peered around Conn's mother and saw a pipe sitting in an ashtray on the small desk under the window.

A used pipe. That was the smell, like one of those old barber-shops-cum-tobacconists dotted around in the towns. The smell of bay rum and tobacco…

Mrs. Bannerman sighed theatrically and shook her head at Conn and Eve. "He thinks I don't know he comes in here to smoke." She frowned at her husband again. "You promised to throw that filthy thing away."

Conn flicked an amused glance at Eve, still holding the rugby ball, then made a passing motion without actually letting go of it. "Reckon you could still throw a ball, old man?"

Mrs. Bannerman's mouth dropped open. Her husband stared at Conn, and Eve saw where his inscrutable expression originated. With a nod he turned and walked out the door, his son on his heels.

The older woman's eyes glistened. "They used to spend hours with that ball," she murmured, as if to herself. "I would yell myself hoarse at dinnertime. More than once I scraped their dinners into the bin, they took so long coming in."

They left soon after and drove back to the city. He spoke little and Eve worried that her indiscretion had irked him. "I'm sorry for putting my foot in it."

He did not reply.

"My gaff about your bedroom?" she reminded him.

"I've just had my thirty-first birthday, Eve. I'm sure they won't be shocked to know I occasionally share my bed."

Maybe not. But Eve realized it wasn't his parents' opinion about her staying over in Conn's room that was important. Suddenly she needed to know what *he* thought about it.

"I suppose I should think about going home." Light and breezy, and only a little nervous.

"You went home yesterday."

She glanced at his profile then quickly back to the road. That was not what she meant—and he knew it. The interest in Eve had died down now that Scanlon was off the front page. There hadn't been a car outside her gate for days.

The silence was long. She shifted in her seat. That was it?

Finally he spoke. "We'll talk about it after the election."

Her breath inched out, drop by drop. It was a reprieve, if only temporary. She had a few days' grace, a few more days to hope that she would become as vital to him as he was becoming to her.

Conn stood on the deck, watching the snow-white throat feathers of a tui flitting through the pohutakawas that clung drunkenly to the cliff face.

"That was fun," Eve had gone to freshen up and now moved close, sliding her arms around his middle from behind. "What's with you and your family?"

He raised his head, frowning out into the gathering gloom. "It's…complicated."

"Because of the accident?"

Conn shrugged out of her embrace and leaned his forearms on the railing. It wasn't that he didn't want to tell her. It just all seemed so maudlin, so distant on the tongue but always too close in his mind. He knew she would understand, not pass judgment. In fact, he knew he could count on her support.

But what did that matter when it was he himself who stuck the knife in? His own self-disgust had made him withdraw from the family he loved, even though he knew it hurt them.

He had lost control. Rachel had died. No matter how much money he made, how spectacular his achievements, he felt he was still rotten to the core.

"The accident was tough on them. They copped a lot of flak. I hated watching it. The more they tried to include and support me, the more I hated it."

He ventured a look at Eve. A quiet reassurance or understanding in her face dislodged the words from his throat, where they had stuck for so long.

"We were at a restaurant," he told the night air. "It was a terrible night, bucketing down. Someone inside must have tipped the photographers off. She went out first and walked right into them." He swore under his breath. "They wouldn't back off and I got rough, a bit of pushing and shoving—not for the first time. I felt like turning the car on them."

A sourness burned his throat. He could almost taste the satisfaction of plowing into them, mowing them down like pins in a bowling alley.

That was his shame, his loss of control.

Somehow his brain had held on to a shred of reason and he'd swerved before hitting anyone. He could have handled the big motor, even though he was just a kid. He could have handled the treacherous conditions. He could have handled his anger at the photographers. He could even have handled his shame at hurting the beautiful girl beside him in such a callous manner.

But he wasn't mature enough to handle all of it at the same time.

Tires screeching, he'd slammed the accelerator to the floor. They'd only gone a couple of hundred meters when he skidded and slammed into a concrete wall. "We were in the car just seconds. Such a short ride to hell."

He heard Eve's shattered breath escape and threw her a glance. Damn woman was crying. He shook his head in disgust.

She confounded him further when she pushed herself into his side and wiped her wet cheek on his shirtsleeve. His body tensed. He turned toward the house abruptly, making her lurch a little as she was left without support. "Want a drink?"

Sniffing, she shook her head. Conn took his time, not bothering with ice. He poured a large bourbon and downed half of it before he turned back to her. The liquor collided with the acid bitterness in his gut, burning a hole a car could drive through. He glared as he approached, daring her to offer sympathy. Tell him as he'd been told a hundred times that it wasn't his fault. A tragic accident. Could have happened to anyone. Get over it…

She faced him, leaning back on the railing with her arms folded and one dainty bare ankle crossed over the other. He remembered those ridiculous socks she'd worn the night he got her out of her sick bed. The night they met.

He wished he didn't have to remember anything that came before they met.

"Go on," she murmured.

He blinked. Go on? Where were his platitudes? Feeling cheated he scowled and neatly took care of the other half of his drink. "The fuss subsided after a while. I had a few operations, slowly recuperated. Then the court case came around and I was front-page news again. Convicted and discharged. The media were outraged.

"As soon as that died down, they aired the last show Rachel ever taped. My folks got hate mail." He rolled the cold glass over his jaw. "I hated watching what it did to them. One day I decided I wasn't going to do it anymore. So I distanced myself."

"That's what families do," she told him gently. "They support you."

Sounds like something she'd say, he thought disparagingly.

"What about Erin, your sister?" she asked.

"She and Rachel were close."

After the accident, Erin told him Rachel had called her on the way out of the restaurant. "The bastard just dumped me," her friend had sobbed. Despite his injuries, his sister was disgusted with him. She later said sorry for going off at him. Shock and grief had made her lash out.

Conn sucked it down, the mushy bruised part of him that missed Erin like hell. They had never regained their bond.

"Did Rachel's parents come to see you?"

"God no." For which he was vehemently grateful. It was bad enough seeing them in court months later.

"Did you go to her funeral?"

Okay, she was being pushy now. Enough with the questions. He banged his empty glass down on the railing and glowered at her. "No, Eve, I didn't go to her funeral. I was in intensive care. What else do you want to know?"

Eve's gaze was unflinching. "I want to know everything."

He shook his head, stopped the bitter laughter that wanted to erupt. "I don't think you do."

"I want to know how you felt about her, then and now."

Her gaze was clear and completely devoid of condemnation or pity. Did she not know how she was supposed to react?

"I was nineteen years old when we met. How do you think nineteen-year-old boys feel about girls, Eve?"

She made no response to his deliberately icy tone. She didn't stop searching his face, either.

"They want to score. That's about it." Conn carefully put very little emphasis on his words, hoping to shock her just a little.

It didn't work. She rubbed her chin, much in the way he did sometimes when trying to wrangle an errant thought to the surface.

"So it wasn't a serious thing for you?"

Conn just stared at her moodily.

"The newspapers said you were devastated. Family and friends said you were in love."

He bit down on the inside of his mouth, relishing the spurt of warm pain. "You don't want to believe everything you read in the papers."

They stared at each other. It was a standoff. Eve looked away first. "Conn, I'm comfortable living with the ghost of a woman you loved. I wouldn't want to usurp or diminish that in any way."

What was she saying? She loved him? Conn swallowed, the wonder of it was short-lived when he remembered that he did not deserve that, did not deserve her. Would not sully her.

"But there is more here than you're saying. You're not telling it all."

"Bloody reporters," he growled.

"I'm not…

"All right!" A well of anger rose up. "I didn't love her. I was using her." How could he love anyone more than he loved himself? "She didn't want to go out that night. She didn't like going out. It often ended being a circus with the press—or the public."

He hauled one of the heavy wooden deck chairs toward him and sat. Somehow it fitted. She loomed above, looking down on him. "Rachel was a nice person. Insanely popular." Like you, he nearly said. And like you she was unfailingly tolerant and pleasant to people. "She'd always had a good relationship with the press—till I came along. It was me who craved the attention. I wanted to be seen. I didn't want to sit home and eat pizza like she did."

He looked down, scratching his hand. "The coach had

reamed me out, told me if I didn't knuckle down instead of pushing photographers around and being tabloid fodder, I was off the team. I decided to sacrifice Rachel. Tomorrow, I thought, I'm going to eat, sleep and breathe rugby. Tonight, I'm gonna enjoy the fuss."

He remembered looking around at all the eyes on them in the restaurant. It was perfect. "I was half hoping she'd make a scene, call me names." He raised his head, needing to see her disgust. "I was playing a part. A superstar in a country whose collective national psyche depended on whether we won or lost a game."

Eve bit her bottom lip but her gaze was steady.

"But she didn't get mad, didn't make a scene or yell. She just—cried." His voice was hoarse. "I honestly didn't expect that. She sat across from me with tears running down her face. Everyone was looking. The whole place went quiet." There weren't any words to describe that feeling. For damn sure, it was marginally less self-destructive than what went through his mind when he'd woken in the hospital and been told of her death.

The muscles in his jawline clenched over and over. "She got up and ran out." He cleared his throat. "You've met my parents, seen the way they brought me up. All I could think was how ashamed they'd be.

"By the time I had paid and gotten outside, Rachel, still crying, was surrounded by photographers. She tried to walk around them, even swore at them when I appeared. I guess she knew by then what I wanted. Some attention. She was playing a part. They were playing their part, too." He shook his head, looking down at his feet. "It was insane."

He heard her slow breath out, smelled her freshness as

she squatted down in front of him, one hand on the arm of the chair, the other on his thigh.

Her eyes were earnest, her voice insistent. "It was an accident, Conn."

Conn's inhalation was deep and wretched. "What I can't bear is that she went to eternity with my rejection ringing in her ears. I hate that they witnessed that, that I made it so public." His head felt heavy and low. "Most of all, I hate that I lived and she didn't."

She squeezed his thigh hard, forcing him to look at her. "You are *not* a monster."

Wasn't he? He knew one thing. It was his punishment that prevented him from embracing the sort of happiness Eve Drumm offered. He had to find a way to push her away, give this up while he still could.

It was for her own good.

"People like you shouldn't be around people like me." He gripped her wrist, his long fingers circling it easily. "I know *I* can survive. Nice people don't. They get hurt—or worse."

Eleven

It was election day. They went into the village at Eve's insistence. She wanted to post their votes in a sort of ceremony of hope. Then she coaxed him into having brunch in a small café overlooking the beach. Eve sat with her back to the other diners, hoping Conn's face would not be as recognizable as hers, remembering their lovemaking that morning.

She woke him with soft caresses and whispered sighs, and he responded with a sleepy boyish eagerness, still cocooned in half-sleep. She took him into her body, trembling with the need to show him she was his and would always be there.

It was a fine line, the need to show and tell. Words were so stark, they forced decisions, could push him to revert to his habit of closing up. But if her actions could not show him and her body not change his mind, what choice was she left with?

They moved together in flowing and gentle motion. Layer upon layer of tension tightened to a heart-stopping peak, quivering on the edge for moments, then dissolving, engulfing them in ecstasy. She choked back the words her heart begged her to say and buried her face in his throat.

An indefinable knot of worry had lodged under her ribs in the days since he had told her about the accident. Nothing she could identify or put her finger on, just a strange sense that he looked at her differently now. Saw her in a different light, was committing her to memory perhaps.

Conn's foot nudged her under the table. "Earth to Eve."

"Sorry." He was doing his best not to notice the stares of the other diners. Eve appreciated that. The least she could do was pay attention.

"Nervous about the election?"

She nodded, knowing that her disquiet was more to do with the conversation she wanted to have with him later. Her future, choice of career, place of residence, all hinged on whether the man across the table felt the same as she did.

"We did all we could," he murmured. "No point being nervous about something out of our control." He raised his head, signaling to the waiter. "Ready to go?"

As they waited for his credit card to be processed, a man approached and pleasantly offered his best wishes for the stadium. Eve turned to thank him, anticipating Conn's curt response, but was amazed to see a guarded smile on his lips as he nodded at the departing man.

Well, well…was the Ice Man thawing? She leaned forward, casting a surreptitious look over her shoulder. "Cheeky devil. I'll foot trip him and you can kick the be-jeebers out of him while he's down."

Conn gave her a withering look, but then that sulky

mouth she loved so much parted in a resigned grin. "You're a real comedian," he muttered, rising to leave.

They took a walk along the narrow street and it was easy to believe they were a couple as they strolled, talking about nothing very much, as couples do. Once he even grabbed her hand as they crossed the road. She wanted to lace their fingers but thought the action may remind him to pull away. When he released her a minute or two later, her disappointment was eased by the smile he gave her. Two smiles in one morning! Life was good.

But soon enough he told her that Saturday or not, he had work to do. Eve opted to stay in the village and shop for dinner. Perhaps the benefit of a few hours apart would open his eyes and bolster her courage to voice her love.

The election results were on at the end of the evening news, only a five-minute item announcing the results. Since Conn rarely watched TV, Eve decided to make a ridiculous celebration of the whole situation. Homemade pizza, guacamole and beer covered the coffee table, as if they were watching a ball game. "Overkill," Conn mumbled but he dug out a couple of baseball caps and entered into the spirit.

As expected, the incumbent mayor had little opposition now that he had come out publicly in support of the stadium. The other candidate barely raised a ripple. Eve sighed with happy relief, knowing Pete Scanlon would have been a certainty if her contact hadn't come forward.

They toasted each other with beer when the results were confirmed and talked of the schedule for the stadium.

Eve raised her bottle. "Here's to you and the timely completion of Gulf Harbor Stadium."

They touched bottles. She had never seen him looking more relaxed. The warmth in his eyes was like a reward.

"And to you and your publicity machine," he said, leaning forward to kiss her behind her ear. "Perhaps we should name a stand after you."

"You'll have to teach me the intricacies of rugby. I aim to be there at that World Cup Final." Would he catch on that she was alluding to the future? Their future together.

Conn gave her a sexy once-over. "You're a bit of a runt, but I could show you the tackled ball rule."

A rush of heat at the all-male look in his eyes had her rolling the icy bottle around her neck and throat. He had so much sensual power over her at times, and even after nearly two weeks, the intensity and urgency of their love-making had not diminished one jot. His eyes held a pull over her body and senses she just could not deny.

And he was doing it to her now. She sat primly on the edge of the couch, anticipation and indecision vying for ascendancy. Tonight was the night she was going to tell him she loved him, make a case for a future with him. Should they talk now or later?

He reached out to graze her mouth with his knuckle.

Later would do.

The phone rang. He got to his feet, leaving her lips tingling with disappointment.

His expression changed to pleased surprise when he heard the voice on the line. Eve waved a magazine in front of her face, still flushed by his mesmerizing sexual heat.

"When?"

She glanced up, startled by the snap of his voice. His eyes narrowed, he walked over and scooped up the TV remote. "Okay. Don't worry about it."

The television flickered into life.

"Thanks, Mum. Say hi to Dad."

"What's up?" Eve pulled the baseball cap off, lacing her fingers through her hair.

He didn't look at her, intent on the screen. "My mother just saw a promo for Felicity Cork at eight o'clock," he told her distractedly.

Eve wrinkled her nose. She had never seen the *City Lights* show, but knew of its reputation as salacious and cruel. Having met her, Eve did not like the hostess one bit; a blowsy, mutton-dressed-as-lamb loudmouth who thought her opinions counted over anyone else's.

She perched on the edge of the sofa, a whisper of dread creeping up her spine. Conn stood in front of the TV with his back to her.

The show began with an overly lavish soundtrack and Felicity's voice-over: "What are these two famous for?"

Several quick-fire shots of Eve, one of Conn. "More than you might think."

The heavily made-up face with its hawkish features and obscenely red lips appeared. Felicity Cork made up for in venom what she lacked in looks.

"Conner 'Ice' Bannerman swept to fame more than a decade ago when he became the youngest rugby player ever to be selected for New Zealand, following in the footsteps of his father, Gary. He dated popular TV actress Rachel Lee for several months before tragedy struck one wet night. The car he was driving crashed. Rachel was killed instantly. It was suggested that he had been drinking and that press photographers were chasing the car when the accident happened. Bannerman was charged with dangerous driving causing death but got off with a suspended sentence.

"Since those dark days, Bannerman has put the tragedy behind him and built up a huge construction business, here and internationally. On the personal front, the icy tycoon has led a virtual hermitlike existence—till now."

Eve could not see his face but there was a stillness in him, a ramrod spine, tension in his shoulders that kept her from going to him. She tried to swallow her fear. This was the worst possible scenario. Her meddling had exposed him to the public.

Flashes of a young Conn and his beautiful lover in her role on the country's number-one soap opera flickered on the screen. Then the presenter's face appeared again.

"Eve Drumm spent the early part of her career producing TV news in the troubled countries of Eastern Europe and Africa. She was married briefly to BBC anchorman James Summers but they divorced recently. Eve returned to New Zealand three years ago to front her own nightly current affairs show, a position she recently left amid speculation she was fired.

"Eve's show was the catalyst in exposing the fraud perpetrated on prominent businessmen by Pete Scanlon, the now-disgraced mayoral candidate who is facing many charges.

"Intriguingly, Bannerman, Inc. was a staunch supporter of Scanlon and it remains to be seen if the Serious Fraud Office investigating have any interest in talking to the CEO of this huge company.

"It appears, however, that being on opposite sides of the political spectrum is no obstacle to true love. Bannerman and Eve Drumm are said to be—" the woman paused and held up her two index fingers, crooking them in a sarcastic parody of speech marks "—close, and sharing more than a passing interest in civic duty. Sources tell me the pair are spending a lot of time together and planning a wedding. That does surprise us here at *City Lights*. The pair could not be more different socially, with Mr. Gulf Harbor Stadium more likely to punch someone—or run them over—than shake their hand, and Eve being just so... syrupy nice."

Bitch! Eve thought.

Conn said it out loud.

"Anyway, we wish them well and look forward to our wedding invitation. Oh, and Eve..." Eve's eyes were closed in distress but she tensed for the last missive.

"You do the driving, dear, or get that big handsome man of yours to the nearest defensive driving course." The horrible woman snorted.

Funny how your life can change in an instant, how a few well-chosen words can cause so much damage. Eve stared apprehensively at the rigid back in front of her, knowing this was all her fault.

She rose, unsure of what to say or even how to feel. She was angry. Felt cheated. Guilt clawed at the back of her neck like loathsome little bat claws.

Conn's head jerked as if he expected her to touch him and was repelled by the thought of it. "Friend of yours?"

"Not!" She twisted her hands together. "I had nothing to do with it."

He turned and looked at her and where she might have expected anger and disbelief, she found only sadness and regret.

"I know that."

Relief washed through her. It was short-lived.

"The fact remains," Conn said woodenly, "that I am now back in the public eye, my bones to be picked over again." He inhaled deeply. "For my family—and Rachel's—to have to go through it all again."

Eve bit her lip, sympathy spilling out of her eyes. "I'm so sorry," she whispered. "But—it's something and nothing, Conn. It will be forgotten by tomorrow. People aren't interested in what happened ten years ago."

Conn brushed past her and sat on the edge of the sofa, his hands spread squarely on his thighs. He frowned down at his bare feet.

She knew what he was doing. He was building his walls up. Closing her out, like he did to everyone. Eve vacillated between backing off and giving him some space or doing what she really wanted to do and pushing him to see her and let her comfort him.

Making a snap decision, she decided letting him have time and space to maneuver would be the wrong choice. She sat beside him, trying to pick up one of his hands with both of hers.

Conn wouldn't let her. His hand was rigid against his thigh. His biceps bunched with tension.

She gave up and instead laced her fingers into the spread-out webs of his, squeezing gently. "Look at me."

His mouth a grim line, he raised his eyes. Trouble glowed, soul deep. Age-old anger.

The knot in her stomach unraveled with a slide of dread. Eve recognized that what she had been seeing in his eyes the past few days was regret. He looked like a man in the throes of making a distasteful decision—unhappy, severe, unyielding. Even now he was boarding up his heart, retreating to the safety of his symbolic fortress.

Eve bit her lip, trying to think rationally. She wouldn't let it happen. She had shaken his world. He *had* changed. He *had* laughed and helped and respected her and comforted. She wasn't going to let him do the backward slide on her watch.

"I bet you my house that this will all blow over in a couple of days. Conn, it was big news back then. It's not now. There's a whole new generation out there who never heard of Ice Bannerman or Rachel Lee. They have new players and actresses to worry over now."

"Who are we kidding, Eve?"

Light words, but his voice was bleak as bones in the desert.

"Wh-what do you mean?"

"We're from different worlds. I won't live in your fishbowl."

"My fishbowl?"

"You're out there, getting into people's living rooms. But they want to be in *your* living room. That's the price."

"I'm not on TV anymore."

"But you will be. It's what you do."

She sat up straighter, tugging on his set fingers, trying to get him to face her. "Conn, I couldn't care less about presenting. I like being in news but I can do something else—producing."

"Don't! Don't change your life or plan your career around me."

She tugged his hand again, adamant he would hear her and see her. "If you don't want me on TV, I won't be on TV. It wouldn't be any hardship for me."

"Eve—" he rubbed the bridge of his nose with his free hand "—in six months you'll be climbing the walls, bored to tears. Wanting to party and be back in the thick of things."

She stared at him, the fog in her brain clearing. There was more going on here than just his dislike of attention. She saw that he had a list in his head and was determined to tick each item off—each dagger to her heart—in a civilized and organized manner.

"You'll be hurt," he continued, "when I say I don't want to go to this function, that party. We'll rip each other apart."

"I don't believe that for a minute—and neither do you." She had to gather herself, shoot him down before those daggers macerated her heart.

Conn sighed. "Eve, I'm...no good at this. I'm not a team player, not a person you want to share with."

"What part of sharing with me didn't you like first thing this morning?" she demanded, referring to their early-morning loving. Dirty tactics maybe, but he wasn't going to get organized or civilized.

Conn's eyes flashed a warning but he chose not to respond.

The stupid thing was, the excuses he was throwing up were insignificant, things that did not reflect their relationship, what they brought to each other. Security, comfort, support, passion. Light in the shadows. This rubbish he was spouting was not at the heart of the matter.

Eve decided to cut to the chase. "Conn, are you going to go the rest of your life believing everyone judges you on one tragic act a long time ago?"

"That's not it, Eve."

"What then? You push everyone away because you blame yourself for the accident and for rejecting her beforehand. Or is it because you don't feel you were punished enough?"

"Psycho-babble!" The crack of his voice told her she was getting close.

Careful, back up. Pushing too hard would go against her. Wounded souls kicked like the devil when cornered.

But all her strategies were crumbling. A chill that started in her marrow rolled through her like a glacier, relentless and consuming.

Conn leaned well back, putting distance between them.

"I think you have this rosy picture in your head. About us. About happy families."

Yes, yes, you're on the right track. She rocked back and forward, rubbing her arms. "Am I moving too fast for you?"

"I don't have that picture in my head." He paused. "About you."

She blinked several times, unable to tear her eyes from his face. He didn't want her? "I see."

But she didn't see. There had to be some clarification. Or—please God—a smile to reassure her. Her whole argument was based on the absolute belief that after the expected resistance, deep down he wanted the same things she did. She had awakened him to love. She'd seen it in his eyes, face, felt it in his loving arms.

But the terrible confirmation wasn't long coming.

"My picture is much more primitive, I'm afraid. And it doesn't include the sort of future you want or deserve." For a brief moment his mouth softened a little. "I'm not a replacement for your failed marriage or your baby."

Damn the tears filling her eyes, stopping her from reading him. They made her angry, made her want to rip into him. She was fighting for her life here and would do whatever it took...

"I love you, Conn," she told him. "Read my lips. *I. Love. You!*"

She thought she'd seen hard and glittering when he'd taken her to task about her first column. His eyes told her she hadn't reached him yet.

"Want me to sign it?"

Without waiting for him to stop shaking his head, she raised her hands and signed. Emphatic, sharp, her fingers stabbed the air two inches in front of his nose.

He didn't flinch. His withdrawal was complete.

The tears that had been threatening for minutes finally spilled over. "Don't do this. Don't freeze me out," Eve whispered. "I've touched you, I know I have."

He clamped his jaw shut and looked for all the world as if he was grinding his teeth.

"You *do* deserve love. You *do* deserve to be happy." Her voice broke but still she made no effort to wipe away her tears. Embarrassment or fear of being seen as weak did not enter her head. "Don't push me away, Conn, because if you do, you'll be alone forever. You'll never find love."

Conn suddenly reared to his feet, dragging her up with him. "Damn it, Eve! Do you have to make this so hard?" He pushed his face in front of hers, gripping her shoulders tightly.

Shocked, she stared up at him. He had never used his size or strength to intimidate her, not even during the wildest lovemaking.

"Don't you remember what I told you about Rachel? How I used her for sex and attention and then cut her loose? Don't you realize by now what sort of man I am?"

She shook her head in denial, lips moving soundlessly. Hope died in her then, and at the same time, a diamond of hurt formed inside her rib cage. How could she have got it so wrong? It was inconceivable that she would fall in love with a man who had ice water in his veins.

"It's the truth!" he insisted. "I used you. I only kept you around until the election because I felt I owed you."

He released her shoulders abruptly but didn't step back.

"Read my lips, Eve. Sex. Exciting. Uncomplicated. Temporary."

Each word a slap. The pain came and it was agony, as bad as losing the baby. As hopeless as her marriage. As full of regrets as her father's death. Eve slumped and stepped back. She was done. "I'll get my things."

How she turned away and walked out of the room, she didn't know. *Keep moving, keep busy...* Somehow she made it to his bedroom, feeling so brittle, so terribly broken inside she wanted to throw up. Mechanically she filled the rucksack she'd used to transport her clothes and then took one long, last look at his bedroom.

Countless kisses and climaxes and touches whispered in the air. Waking up and rolling into his side, seeing his sleepy welcoming smile, the smile of a new day with her beside him, before he remembered all the bad in the world.

Eve straightened her spine. Now wasn't the time to break down. It was time to gather the shredded remains of her dignity. Keep moving. Get out of here. She hoisted up her rucksack.

Conn waited by the door, his car keys in his hand. They didn't speak. A couple of minutes later he stopped outside her house.

This was it. Over. The skin on her cheeks was tight and burning. She wouldn't look at him again, couldn't bear to see pity in his eyes. Couldn't bear not to.

She opened the door.

"I'm sorry if..." His voice trailed off. He couldn't even finish an apology, that's how little regard he had for her.

Her heart hardened. She hauled the rucksack from the floor of the car. "I'm sorry, too," she muttered, not caring if he heard clearly or not. "For you, for what you're going to feel. For the bleak future ahead of you."

Eve slammed the car door and stalked up her path without looking back. But her heart was breaking.

Most of all, she was just sorry for herself.

Twelve

The stretch of beach was on an isolated part of the island, and he ran and ran until his knee gave out. The sand was wet, and he sat there cursing at the pain that crunched and grabbed. His doctors had told him the reconstruction would only last so long, he would likely have to have more surgery one day.

It was brain surgery he needed.

This was the second day since his mauling of her, and not a word from her. Was she feeling this bad? He couldn't imagine it. But then, he was the one who had wielded the sword.

Conn had spent the first night sitting at his table, staring at her house. The lights had burned all through the night. He was still there when a taxi pulled up at first light. She carried out a suitcase and rucksack. He imagined her smiling at the driver. Would she always present a bright facade, even after the damage he'd done?

He told himself over and over he'd done it for her own good. Ripped her heart out, sliced her into ribbons. Told himself that all the reasons why they shouldn't be together were valid—except for the last.

The letter from her lawyer was hand delivered two days later. She would accept his offer to buy her house but she'd upped the price an extra ten thousand dollars.

He rang the lawyer, demanding to know where she was. The man was reticent until Conn threatened to scuttle the deal unless he spoke to her.

She called. No pleasantries, no hello. "You once said I was a nice person with a streak of sado-masochism," she told him in a curt voice. "I must be. I'm talking to you."

"Where are you?"

She hesitated, probably thinking what the hell was it to do with him. "I'm staying with my mother for a while."

"This island is big enough for both of us. I don't know why you feel you have to sell up."

"Don't you?"

Of course he did. "No, I don't."

"You want me to tell you?"

No, he didn't. "If you want to."

He listened to her working up to it. The in-drawn jagged breath. The sound of sadness.

"I can't live next to you, loving you, knowing you don't feel the same way."

"Why does it have to be all or nothing," Conn exploded. "And why do you have to push so hard?" His lungs felt like they were bursting. He was furious with her for leaving, with himself for hurting her. For losing her. The defeat in her voice punished him.

Eve's response was a long time coming, and cool. "I

don't recall asking for everything *right now*. Just a hint that you might consider it one day, that's all."

"Consider what?"

She paused. "You. Me. Babies." He heard her shaky intake of breath. "Living."

The silence yawned down the line.

"Take the deal, Conn. You're getting a bargain. Send the contract to my mother's address." She gave the details and hung up without saying goodbye.

The hum down the line roared in his head. Finally his brain kicked into gear. About ninth gear, obviously. "I love you too, Eve," he said aloud. "I don't want you to go."

She moved fast. The following day the furniture truck was there. Conn kept the binoculars trained all day, looking for her. She wasn't there.

It was so damn quiet! He slid one of the CDs she'd left into the stereo, poured himself a drink and stood on the deck, watching her house going nowhere. Like his life. Perversely he walked to the stereo and turned the volume up to a ridiculous level—ridiculous to anyone but Eve Drumm.

Sometime in the next couple of days, he found himself inside her empty house. He wandered around, touching surfaces, breathing her in. Cursing her. He'd known her little more than a month. How had he gone ten years without any emotional involvement and now be sleepless and unable to work?

It made him wonder what he had ever found pleasure in over the past decade—and why that pleasure eluded him now.

He tried to work but it was too quiet. He hated going to

bed alone, yet worse was the way his heart slammed him every single morning, waking without her. He didn't shave. He looked like hell. Every time he began to scrub potatoes, took steak from the freezer—he would end up eating another cardboard sandwich, aware of a gnawing hunger but too uninterested to rectify it.

After yet another sleepless night, he picked up the phone. "Phyll? Get me a wrecking crew out here."

Legally he didn't have a leg to stand on. Eve could sue his ass off since he did not actually own the house yet.

He hoped she would.

He watched from the window as the bulldozer rolled down her drive, then suddenly he was up and limping to his car.

"Don't touch the letterbox. When the rest of it is rubble, dig it up. Bring it to my house. And be careful with it."

Con assumed his position in front of the window and took up the binoculars for his own private show. His heart shattered into tiny pieces like the walls and the roof of the old Baxter place.

She gave into it after church, while visiting the cemetery with her mother. Sinking to her knees in the damp grass, she hugged herself, rocking back and forth. Her mother's legs pressed into her back while the pain tore about inside her, raging, like a nightmare horror movie.

When would she learn to defend herself? It wasn't as if she had gone into it with her eyes closed, blissfully igno- rant of the probable consequences.

Didn't stop her though…

Packing, transportation, storage. Long talks with her mother and reunions with old friends—Eve had crammed a lot into the past week. But it was always lurking at the dark edges of her mind. Now here, in the tranquility of the cemetery, with her family's love supporting her, the grief had to come out.

The release was kind of cathartic. After the flood of tears eased, she hoped the worst was over. Please God.

Her mother passed a wad of tissues over her shoulder. Eve mopped her face, then reached out and cleaned the headstone.

"Here lies Frank Drumm," she read aloud, just to hear a voice. "Much-loved husband of Mary and father of Evangeline."

And underneath. "Here lies Beth Summers, much-loved daughter of James and Evangeline (Eve) Summers (nee Drumm) and loved granddaughter of Mary and the late Frank Drumm."

Eve had carried the ashes of her daughter all the way from London, thought she would always keep them with her. But when her father died, she couldn't bear for him—or Beth—to be alone.

Alone. Her mother walked beside her, squeezing her arm periodically, but Eve still felt so alone.

She had been roped in to help at the monthly Deaf Association Sunday lunch. She smiled and signed, translating the orders from the dozen deaf diners to the wait staff. The Mackay Working Men's Club Sunday lunches were popular, and the place was rocking.

Yesterday she'd had a phone call from one of the directors of her old TV station. It was a greatly improved offer, one of several she was considering. But she was fairly clear on one thing. Presenting wasn't her future.

Personally, her options were not as clear. She didn't want to discover in five years time that her body could not support and nurture a baby. Maybe she would look for a nice country man who would cherish her and give her the babies she desired.

And there would be no lust. Eve had had two disastrous relationships based on lust. Next time if there was even an inkling of it, she would fly like the wind.

Her mother winked at her over ancient Mrs. Pembroke's head. Could she stay here? It was something, to be co-cooned in the familiarity and quiet of a country town after the rigors of the last year or so. Something, too, to be close to her father and baby. Eve had to consider that her mum wasn't getting any younger and would never leave Mackay, with a strong and supportive network of friends here.

Someone asked about dessert, and Eve took their orders, going around the table with her notepad. A blast of cold air and a large figure in a long black overcoat attracted the attention of several of her charges. She looked up and froze, her fingers contorted in midair.

Conn Bannerman's eyes zoned in on her instantly.

Gaunt. Unshaven. Ominous. His eyes slayed her at twenty paces. As he closed the distance, worry gripped her with icy fingers. His healthy tan had faded, and she was seared by his haunted eyes.

Had someone died?

He stopped about three feet away. "Can we talk?" More of a hoarse demand than a request.

Eve's spine went rigid with dread. "What's happened?" she choked out. "Your mother?"

Both hands raised up quickly, as if she'd pulled a gun on him. "Nothing like that."

She deflated with a long breath of relief. Okay. What else? Maybe the house had burned down.

Conn cast a pained look at the table of diners. "Privately?"

Now that her worry had cleared, the hurt and indignation took hold. Her head lifted. "They can't hear you." She felt the curious stares of several pair of eyes. Someone had better come up with one good reason why she should even give him the time of day.

His eyes flicked around the table. He looked very ill at ease.

"How did you know to come here?"

"The guy at the gas station," he told her cryptically.

Eve looked through the window to the parking lot and easily picked out the big black Mercedes. She started. The Merc, not the limo. His private car.

No wonder he looked rattled if he'd driven the length of the country to find her. "Has something gone wrong with the sale?" Anything else was just too overwhelming to contemplate.

Conn passed a weary hand over his face. "You've spoiled everything, you know."

Their eyes met briefly then skittered away but she fancied his mouth was a little less pinched, his eyes a little less tormented than a minute ago. Even so, his halfhearted accusation did not require a response.

"I was happy until you came along."

That did it. "No you weren't."

He sighed. "Well, I didn't know that. I was comfortable. Peaceful."

Someone touched her hand, pointing at an item on the menu. Eve nodded and noted cheesecake on her pad.

"Your problem is," Conn muttered, "you're too alive."

Eve stared hard at the pad, thinking that wasn't the sort of thing one would say about a house deal. She looked up at him. It wasn't the sort of thing Conn Bannerman would say, period.

Anguish stared back at her. Tears sprang into her eyes before she could look away.

"See?" Anguish faded into irritation. "That's exactly what I'm talking about."

He seemed too alive. So, if not a discussion about the house... Eve's heart stuttered.

"I miss that," Conn said softly, "since you left."

"You miss my crying?"

"No!" He shuddered. "God, no."

She swallowed, pushing down a ray of hope. She imagined that hard place inside her, the place she called her scar. In her mind it was shiny, smooth over rough, like ground glass under silk. And if she pressed it—in her mind—it brought the humiliation and the hurt back. A forever reminder.

"I brought the letterbox."

Her head rose. What was he on about now? "In the car? It must weigh a ton."

"It does. So think very carefully about where you want me to lug it to next."

Eve shook her head, bewildered. "I don't have any-where..." At the head of the table, her mother was flicking her fingers, trying to get her attention.

"It looks—" Conn swallowed "—okay at my house." His eyes dropped to her throat. "If you were thinking of..."

Her quick intake of breath was in response to a giddy surge of heartbeat gone wild. Again she crushed it down. Don't presume. Look where presuming got you last time.

Conn's head rolled back. "Or wherever you want."

She shrank her eyes to slits, warning him. "You'd better

start making sense soon. I'm busy." Turning to the table, she clapped her hands. "Come on, people. Let's get this show on the road. Dessert?"

A dozen pairs of eyes gazed from her to Conn and back again. There was an expectant hush, broken by his gusty and slightly impatient sigh.

"You!" he said distinctly, and her head swiveled back to face him. "Me. Babies. Living."

Eve's mouth dropped wide open. His enunciation was perfect. Not one person at this table would have a problem lipreading that.

"That's what you said you wanted, wasn't it?"

The tip of her pencil snapped. She glanced down, but the only words she could decipher were his, at the back of her eyelids. You. Me. Babies. Living.

Eve was mildly asthmatic as a child. Short, shallow breaths, the panicky feeling that she couldn't expel them. Erratic pulse pounding in her ears.

And a letterbox, too! Somebody whack me on the back, please.

Tight-chested, she looked back at Conn's face, searching for the warmth he'd shown glimpses of, or that he believed in a future with her and not just because he'd hurt her. Or even just a sign that he had stopped punishing himself. But since the breakup, any confidence in her ability to read his eyes, his face, had taken a beating. Proceed with caution, she told herself, and that seemed to ease the constriction in her chest. "Does love come into it?"

His shoulders slumped a little. "That much I'm sure of."

Her bottom lip hurt like the devil but she kept her teeth embedded, relishing the pain that told her she wasn't dreaming.

He stepped closer and raised his hand. "Careful."

Eve let him brush her mouth with his thumb. This close, she could almost smell his fatigue and unhappiness. "Does it make you happy, Conn? Loving me?"

The sorrow in his eyes was palpable. "What makes me very unhappy is hurting you like I did." His mouth turned down even more. "I never want to see that look on your face again."

An excellent start. "That's not what I asked."

He looked at her for a long time, as if the very sight of her bolstered him, kept him standing. Eve couldn't help it. She moved toward him just as he reached for her hands, holding them tightly between them.

He swallowed. "When I was cold, you warmed me up," he told her in a clear and somber voice. "When I was empty, you filled me." His eyes flicked self-consciously over the rapt expressions of their audience. "When I couldn't hear, you opened my ears."

Squeezing his hands, Eve thought that was probably the most romantic thing she had ever heard. She blinked against the tears, but they came anyway, and it didn't matter because his eyes were suspiciously brilliant also.

He released her hands and brought his up to cup her face. "You showed me how it could be, how I want it to be." His voice lowered to a hoarse whisper. "I love you, Eve. I don't want to go back."

Her hands closed over his and at the same time he lowered his forehead to rest on hers. He had bared his heart and soul and offered them to her, knowing it was a worthy gift and that she would treat it as such. And he didn't care who knew it. Her heart sang.

Her voice was as low as his. "Then come forward with

me." They stood with just their hands and foreheads touching, breathing in sweat and vanquished despair, relief and love. Eve had found a sort of tranquility at her father's grave this morning and she sank back into it now. And in her mind the scar lost its ragged edges, softened and blurred into nothing.

Then someone tapped her arm and she opened her eyes. Conn released her when the man seated nearest handed her a paper napkin, folded into an airplane. She recognized her mother's scrawl. "Aren't you going to introduce us?"

She turned. The elder Drumm grinned impishly. Eve smiled back and signed, "Wait your patience." Then "What do you think?"

Her mother didn't hesitate. "Very nice," she signed. "A bit wild-eyed, if you know what I mean."

Laughter bubbled up. She nodded her agreement and turned back to her wild-eyed man. "That's my mother." She beamed. "I think she likes you."

Conn was still not completely at ease in this public forum but he did give her mother a polite nod.

"My old house will be perfect for when she comes to visit," she told him happily. "She likes her independence."

Conn blinked rapidly and then cleared his throat. "Or one of the units at my—*our* place. She could be just as independent there."

Our place. "That sounds lovely," she sighed, misty-eyed with joy. She did not need the words, a proposal. To her, they had already said their vows, right here in front of witnesses. The love shining from his suspiciously brilliant, wild-eyed eyes was all she needed.

She moved closer, reaching her arms up to wrap around his neck. "What's a girl got to do to get a kiss around here?"

Conn tried to look scandalized—for about a second. His arms slid around her waist.

There was an eruption of sound—chairs scraping back, cutlery clattering on crockery, applause and laughter swelled. Mostly from the noisy end, her mother's end of the table, Eve guessed. But she could not drag her eyes off Conn's face. "Unless, of course you don't want to be seen kissing a celebrity in the Working Men's Club of Mackay…"

He pressed her closer. The cacophony behind them reached a crescendo. Conn shook his head, his teeth showing in a resigned smile. "Let's give 'em something to talk about," and his lips descended in a triumphant kiss.

* * * * *

*Experience entertaining women's fiction for every
woman who has wondered "what's next?" in their lives.
Turn the page for a sneak preview of a new book
from Harlequin NEXT,
WHY IS MURDER ON THE MENU, ANYWAY?
by Stevi Mittman*

On sale December 26, wherever books are sold.

Ambience is everything. Imagine eating a foie gras at a luncheonette counter or a side of coleslaw at Le Cirque. It's not a matter of food but one of atmosphere. Remember that when planning your dining room design.

—Tips from *Teddi.com*

"Now that's the kind of man you should be looking for," my mother, the self-appointed keeper of my shelf-life stamp, says. She points with her fork at a man in the corner of the Steak-Out Restaurant, a dive I've just been hired to redecorate. Making this restaurant look four-star will be hard, but not half as hard as getting through lunch without strangling the woman across the table from me. "*He* would make a good husband."

"Oh, you can tell that from across the room?" I ask, wondering how it is she can forget that when we had trouble getting rid of my last husband, she shot him. "Besides being ten minutes away from death if he actually eats all that steak, he's twenty years too old for me and— shallow woman that I am—twenty pounds too heavy. Besides, I am *so* not looking for another husband here. I'm looking to design a new image for this place, looking for some sense of ambience, some ·feeling, something I can build a proposal on for them."

My mother studies the man in the corner, tilting her head, the better to gauge his age, I suppose. I think she's grimacing, but with all the Botox and Restylane injected into that face, it's hard to tell. She takes another bite of her steak salad, chews slowly so that I don't miss the fact that the steak is a poor cut and tougher than it should be. "You're concentrating on the wrong kind of proposal," she says finally. "Just look at this place, Teddi. It's a dive. There are hardly any other diners. What does *that* tell you about the food?"

"That they cater to a dinner crowd and it's lunchtime," I tell her.

I don't know what I was thinking bringing her here with me. I suppose I thought it would be better than eating alone. There really are days when my common sense goes on vacation. Clearly, this is one of them. I mean, really, did I not resolve less than three weeks ago that I would not let my mother get to me anymore?

What good are New Year's resolutions, anyway?

Mario approaches the man's table and my mother

studies him while they converse. Eventually Mario leaves
the table with a huff, after which the diner glances up and
meets my mother's gaze. I think she's smiling at him. That
or she's got indigestion. They size each other up.

I concentrate on making sketches in my notebook and
try to ignore the fact that my mother is flirting. At nearly
seventy, she's developed an unhealthy interest in members
of the opposite sex to whom she isn't married.

According to my father, who has broken the TMI rule
and given me Too Much Information, she has no interest
in sex with him. Better, I suppose, to be clued in on what
they aren't doing in the bedroom than have to hear what
they might be doing.

"He's not so old," my mother says, noticing that I have
barely touched the Chinese chicken salad she warned me
not to get. "He's got about as many years on you as you
have on your little cop friend."

She does this to make me crazy. I know it, but it works
all the same. "Drew Scoones is not my little 'friend.' He's
a detective with whom I—"

"Screwed around," my mother says. I must look
shocked, because my mother laughs at me and asks if I
think she doesn't know the "lingo."

What I thought she didn't know was that Drew and I
actually tangled in the sheets. And, since it's possible she's
just fishing, I sidestep the issue and tell her that Drew is
just a couple of years younger than me and that I don't need
reminding. I dig into my salad with renewed vigor, determined to show my mother that Chinese chicken salad in a
steak place was not the stupid choice it's proving to be.

After a few more minutes of my picking at the wilted
leaves on my plate, the man my mother has me nearly

engaged to pays his bill and heads past us toward the back of the restaurant. I watch my mother take in his shoes, his suit and the diamond pinkie ring that seems to be cutting off the circulation in his little finger.

"Such nice hands," she says after the man is out of sight. "Manicured." She and I both stare at my hands. I have two popped acrylics that are being held on at weird angles by bandages. My cuticles are ragged and there's marker decorating my right hand from measuring carelessly when I did a drawing for a customer.

Twenty minutes later she's disappointed that he managed to leave the restaurant without our noticing. He will join the list of the ones I let get away. I will hear about him twenty years from now when—according to my mother—my children will be grown and I will still be single, living pathetically alone with several dogs and cats.

After my ex, that sounds good to me.

The waitress tells us that our meal has been taken care of by the management and, after thanking Mario, the owner, complimenting him on the wonderful meal and assuring him that once I have redecorated his place people will be flocking here in droves (I actually use those words and ignore my mother when she rolls her eyes), my mother and I head for the restroom.

My father—unfortunately not with us today—has the patience of a saint. He got it over the years of living with my mother. She, perhaps as a result, figures he has the patience for both of them, and feels justified having none. For her, no rules apply, and a little thing like a picture of a man on the door to a public restroom is certainly no barrier to using the john. In all fairness, it does seem silly to stand and wait for the ladies' room if no one is using the men's room.

Still, it's the idea that rules don't apply to her, signs don't apply to her, conventions don't apply to her. She knocks on the door to the men's room. When no one answers she gestures to me to go in ahead. I tell her that I can certainly wait for the ladies' room to be free and she shrugs and goes in herself.

Not a minute later there is a bloodcurdling scream from behind the men's room door.

"Mom!" I yell. "Are you all right?"

Mario comes running over, the waitress on his heels. Two customers head our way while my mother continues to scream.

I try the door, but it is locked. I yell for her to open it and she fumbles with the knob. When she finally manages to unlock and open it, she is white behind her two streaks of blush, but she is on her feet and appears shaken but not stirred.

"What happened?" I ask her. So do Mario and the waitress and the few customers who have migrated to the back of the place.

She points toward the bathroom and I go in, thinking it serves her right for using the men's room. But I see nothing amiss.

She gestures toward the stall, and, like any self-respecting and suspicious woman, I poke the door open with one finger, expecting the worst.

What I find is worse than the worst.

The husband my mother picked out for me is sitting on the toilet. His pants are puddled around his ankles, his hands are hanging at his sides. Pinned to his chest is some sort of Health Department certificate.

Oh, and there is a large, round, bloodless bullet hole between his eyes.

Four Nassau County police officers are securing the area, waiting for the detectives and crime scene personnel to show up. They are trying, though not very hard, to comfort my mother, who in another era would be considered to be suffering from the vapors. Less tactful in the twenty-first century, I'd say she was losing it. That is, if I didn't know her better, know she was milking it for everything it was worth.

My mother loves attention. As it begins to flag, she swoons and claims to feel faint. Despite four No Smoking signs, my mother insists it's all right for her to light up because, after all, she's in shock. Not to mention that signs, as we know, don't apply to her.

When asked not to smoke, she collapses mournfully in a chair and lets her head loll to the side, all without mussing her hair.

Eventually, the detectives show up to find the four patrolmen all circled around her, debating whether to administer CPR, smelling salts or simply call the paramedics. I, however, know just what will snap her to attention.

"Detective Scoones," I say loudly. My mother parts the sea of cops.

"We have to stop meeting like this," he says lightly to me, but I can feel him checking me over with his eyes, making sure I'm all right while pretending not to care.

"What have you got in those pants?" my mother asks him, coming to her feet and staring at his crotch accusingly.

"*Baydar?* Everywhere we Bayers are, you turn up. You don't expect me to buy that this is a coincidence, I hope."

Drew tells my mother that it's nice to see her, too, and asks if it's his fault that her daughter seems to attract disasters.

Charming to be made to feel like the bearer of a plague. He asks how I am.

"Just peachy," I tell him. "I seem to be making a habit of finding dead bodies, my mother is driving me crazy and the catering hall I booked two freakin' years ago for Dana's bat mitzvah has just been shut down by the Board of Health!"

"Glad to see your luck's finally changing," he says, giving me a quick squeeze around the shoulders before turning his attention to the patrolmen, asking what they've got, whether they've taken any statements, moved anything, all the sort of stuff you see on TV, without any of the drama. That is, if you don't count my mother's threats to faint every few minutes when she senses no one's paying attention to her.

Mario tells his waitstaff to bring everyone espresso, which I decline because I'm wired enough. Drew pulls him aside and a minute later I'm handed a cup of coffee that smells divinely of Kahlúa.

The man knows me well. Too well.

His partner, whom I've met once or twice, says he'll interview the kitchen staff. Drew asks Mario if he minds if he takes statements from the patrons first and gets to him and the waitstaff afterward.

"No, no," Mario tells him. "Do the patrons first." Drew raises his eyebrow at me like he wants to know if I get the double entendre. I try to look bored.

"What is it with you and murder victims?" he asks me when we sit down at a table in the corner.

I search them out so that I can see you again, I almost say, but I'm afraid it will sound desperate instead of sarcastic.

My mother, lighting up and daring him with a look to tell her not to, reminds him that *she* was the one to find the body.

Drew asks what happened *this time*. My mother tells him how the man in the john was "taken" with me, couldn't take his eyes off me and blatantly flirted with both of us. To his credit, Drew doesn't laugh, but his smirk is undeniable to the trained eye. And I've had my eye trained on him for nearly a year now.

"While he was noticing you," he asks me, "did *you* notice anything about him? Was he waiting for anyone? Watching for anything?"

I tell him that he didn't appear to be waiting or watching. That he made no phone calls, was fairly intent on eating and did, indeed, flirt with my mother. This last bit Drew takes with a grain of salt, which was the way it was intended.

"And he had a short conversation with Mario," I tell him. "I think he might have been unhappy with the food, though he didn't send it back."

Drew asks what makes me think he was dissatisfied, and I tell him that the discussion seemed acrimonious and that Mario looked distressed when he left the table. Drew makes a note and says he'll look into it and asks about anyone else in the restaurant. Did I see anyone who didn't seem to belong, anyone who was watching the victim, anyone looking suspicious?

"Besides my mother?" I ask him, and Mom huffs and blows her cigarette smoke in my direction.

I tell him that there were several deliveries, the kitchen staff going in and out the back door to grab a smoke. He stops me and asks what I was doing checking out the back door of the restaurant.

Proudly—because, while he was off forgetting me, dropping by only once in a while to say hi to Jesse, my son, or drop something by for one of my daughters that he thought they might like, I was getting on with my life—I tell him that I'm decorating the place.

He looks genuinely impressed. "Commercial customers? That's great," he says. Okay, that's what he *ought* to say. What he actually says is "Whatever pays the bills."

"Howard Rosen, the famous restaurant critic, got her the job," my mother says. "You met him—the good-looking, distinguished gentleman with the *real* job, something to be proud of. I guess you've never read his reviews in *Newsday*."

Drew, without missing a beat, tells her that Howard's reviews are on the top of his list, as soon as he learns how to read.

"I only meant—" my mother starts, but both of us assure her that we know just what she meant.

"So," Drew says. "Deliveries?"

I tell him that Mario would know better than I, but that I saw vegetables come in, maybe fish and linens.

"This is the second restaurant job Howard's got her," my mother tells Drew.

"At least she's getting *something* out of the relationship," he says.

"If he were here," my mother says, ignoring the insinuation, "he'd be comforting her instead of interrogating her. He'd be making sure we're both all right after such an ordeal."

"I'm sure he would," Drew agrees, then looks me in the

eyes as if he's measuring my tolerance for shock. Quietly he adds, "But then maybe he doesn't know just what strong stuff your daughter's made of."

It's the closest thing to a tender moment I can expect from Drew Scoones. My mother breaks the spell. "She gets that from me," she says.

Both Drew and I take a minute, probably to pray that's all I inherited from her.

"I'm just trying to save you some time and effort," my mother tells him. "My money's on Howard."

Drew withers her with a look and mutters something that sounds suspiciously like "fool's gold." Then he excuses himself to go back to work.

I catch his sleeve and ask if it's all right for us to leave. He says sure, he knows where we live. I say goodbye to Mario. I assure him that I will have some sketches for him in a few days, all the while hoping that this murder doesn't cancel his redecorating plans. I need the money desperately, the alternative being borrowing from my parents and being strangled by the strings.

My mother is strangely quiet all the way to her house. She doesn't tell me what a loser Drew Scoones is—despite his good looks—and how I was obviously drooling over him. She doesn't ask me where Howard is taking me tonight or warn me not to tell my father about what happened because he will worry about us both and no doubt insist we see our respective psychiatrists.

She fidgets nervously, opening and closing her purse over and over again.

"You okay?" I ask her. After all, she's just found a dead man on the toilet, and tough as she is that's got to be upsetting.

When she doesn't answer me I pull over to the side of the road.

"Mom?" She refuses to meet my eyes. "You want me to take you to see Dr. Cohen?"

She looks out the window as if she's just realized we're on Broadway in Woodmere. "Aren't we near Marvin's Jewelers?" she asks, pulling something out of her purse.

"What have you got, Mother?" I ask, prying open her fingers to find the murdered man's ring.

"It was on the sink," she says in answer to my dropped jaw. "I was going to get his name and address and have you return it to him so that he could ask you out. I thought it was a sign that the two of you were meant to be together."

"He's dead, Mom. You understand that, right?" I ask. You never can tell when my mother is fine and when she's in la-la land.

"Well, I didn't know that," she shouts at me. "Not at the time."

I ask why she didn't give it to Drew, realize that she wouldn't give Drew the time in a clock shop and add, "…or one of the other policemen?"

"For heaven's sake," she tells me. "The man is dead, Teddi, and I took his ring. How would that look?"

Before I can tell her it looks just the way it is, she pulls out a cigarette and threatens to light it.

"I mean, really," she says, shaking her head like it's my brains that are loose. "What does he need with it now?"

In February, expect **MORE**
from

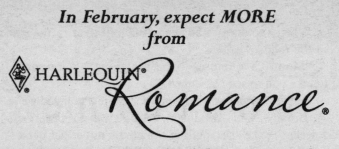

HARLEQUIN® *Romance®*

as it increases to six titles per month.

What's to come...

Rancher and Protector

Part of the
Western Weddings
miniseries

BY JUDY CHRISTENBERRY

The Boss's Pregnancy Proposal

BY RAYE MORGAN

Don't miss February's
incredible line up of authors!

www.eHarlequin.com

nocturne™

**WAS HE HER SAVIOR
OR HER NIGHTMARE?**

HAUNTED
LISA CHILDS

Years ago, Ariel and her sisters were separated for
their own protection. Now the man who vowed
revenge on her family has resumed the hunt, and
Ariel must warn her sisters before it's too late.
The closer she comes to finding them, the more
secretive her fiancé becomes. Can she trust the man
she plans to spend eternity with? Or has he been
waiting for the perfect moment to destroy her?

On sale December 2006.

Silhouette

SPECIAL EDITION™

Logan's Legacy Revisited

**THE LOGAN FAMILY IS BACK
WITH SIX NEW STORIES.**

Beginning in January 2007 with

THE COUPLE
MOST LIKELY TO

by

LILIAN DARCY

Tragedy drove them apart. Reunited eighteen
years later, their attraction was once again
undeniable. But had time away changed
Jake Logan enough to let him face his fears
and commit to the woman he once loved?

REQUEST YOUR FREE BOOKS!

2 FREE NOVELS PLUS 2 FREE GIFTS!

Silhouette® Desire®

Passionate, Powerful, Provocative!

Two classic romances from
New York Times bestselling author

DEBBIE MACOMBER

Damian Dryden. *Ready for romance?* At the age of fourteen, Jessica was wildly infatuated with Evan Dryden. But that was just a teenage crush and now, almost ten years later, she's in love—truly in love—with his older brother, Damian. But everyone, including Damian, believes she's still carrying a torch for Evan.

Evan Dryden. *Ready for marriage?* Mary Jo is the woman in love with Evan. But her background's blue collar, while Evan's is blue blood. So three years ago, she got out of his life—and broke his heart. Now she needs his help. More than that, she wants his love.

The Dryden brothers—bachelors no longer. Not if these women have anything to say about it!

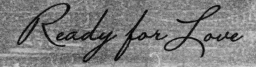

Ready for Love

Debbie Macomber "has a gift for evoking the emotions that are at the heart of the [romance] genre's popularity."
—*Publishers Weekly*

Available the first week of December 2006, wherever paperbacks are sold!

MIRA®

Don't miss
DAKOTA FORTUNES,
a six-book continuing series following
the Fortune family of South Dakota—
oil is in their blood and privilege
is their birthright.

This series kicks off with
USA TODAY bestselling author
PEGGY MORELAND'S
Merger of Fortunes
(SD #1771)
this January.